# The Sour Taste of Suspicion

by CeeCee James

Dedicated to my precious family. 333

Table of Contents

# Chapter 1

Elise's stomach growled, not in the *give me a candy bar, I missed lunch* kind of way, but in the *you feed me ramen noodles again I'm going to revolt.* She walked into the kitchen and threw open the cupboard. Sighing, she pushed around the same packages of ramen purchased in bulk from the Mart Club. She slammed the door shut, her bottom lip doing its nervous habit of finding its way between her teeth. *Dog walking is not cutting it any more.* With a groan, she sank into a kitchen chair and dragged over her laptop. After a few clicks, she pulled up the help wanted list.

There were a few jobs there in her town but the problem was she lacked experience for most of them. Her marriage of ten years had recently ended when her ex-husband chose to have an affair. And now here she was at thirty-three, trying to start over.

Looking down the list of jobs, her brow wrinkled as she ticked them off. Dental Assistant. Nurse. Middle School Teacher. Bus Driver. CPA. *Nope. Nope. Nope.* She rubbed her forehead. I*'ve got to figure this out. What am I going to do?*

*Brrrrit!* A soft meow made Elise glance up at the china buffet. Curled on top was her orange cat, Max. His tail lashed against the ornate wood trim and he slit his eyes when he noticed her staring.

"Max! What are you doing? You know you aren't supposed to sleep up there."

He sat and began washing his face at her words, paw working carefully over his cheek and ear.

Elise closed her eyes. "Lovely, even my cat dismisses me."

The clock chimed twelve, reminding her it was time to get out there and walk the dogs. *Hey. At least it pays for another night of yellow, salty noodles.* Her stomach clenched again at the thought.

Elise searched for her sneakers as she mentally checked off her chore list. Cat fed? Check. Dishes? Done. Bills paid? Hysterical laughter. She tied her shoes and scooped her brown hair up into a ponytail. A smile flickered across her lips as she smoothed the hair back. Lavina, her best friend since grade school, had been so upset that summer to discover a few gray hairs amongst her brilliantly red hair. "Elise!" Lavina had shouted. "It's not fair! Why don't you have any? Your hair is still as dark as a nut-like as it's always been." Elise had shrugged and told Lavina just to pull it out. Lavina's eyes had gone wide at the suggestion. "You want to ruin me? Don't you know if you pull out a gray you get two more?"

Still smiling, as she often did when it came to Lavina, Elise grabbed her phone and keys from the counter and headed for the front door. As she was locking it, her cell rang.

"Lady! Where are you this very minute?" A frantic voice blasted out.

Elise laughed. "Lavina, I swear, I was just thinking about you."

"I must have been shooting you mind bullets. I have an emergency!"

"What's the emergency?"

"My Aunt Myrtle called me this morning at six am. She has a job for me!"

*Oh. Not a real emergency.* Elise started a light jog to the first house where a Pekingese waited. "You were up that early and you're still alive?" Elise snorted. She knew how Lavina detested waking up early.

"It's not funny. That woman has called me three more times since then. She was my grandma's sister, and you know how that generation is about family obligation."

"What job does she want you to do?"

"She wants a companion for a few weeks. Of course I thought of you."

"Me? What?"

"Yes! You'd be perfect! And you'll love it! She has the most beautiful mansion called Montgomery Manor.

You'd have the run of it, with servants to help you with anything you could ever possibly need. She just needs someone to stay with her until her niece finishes her semester at school."

"What about you?"

Lavina paused dramatically. "Elise. You know I couldn't possibly stay all the way out there. I have my deli to run. And what would Mr. G think? Besides, if you absolutely hate it, I'll find someone else. But just do one week for me. Please?"

Elise rolled her eyes. Technically, she owed Lavina a favor for taking her on a cruise last summer. And Mr. G's identity was so secretive, even Elise didn't know who he was. "Um...."

"Plus the job offers a thousand dollars a week."

*Well, now, that certainly changes things.* After all, it *was* perfect timing since her dog walking was about to be on a lull. Mrs. Campbell was a snow bird and Elise was sure Rose would let her off walking the Pekingese for a short while.

"I'll do it." Elise said.

"Lovely! Just one little thing."

"What?" Elise's chest tightened.

"She's crazy," Lavina said before ringing off.

# Chapter 2

Elise drove her tiny Pinto along the country road, already eight miles from town. The houses along this road were old and sprawling. Several had massive gates, locking them safely away from the main road behind wrought iron fences. She looked down to check her directions and then the road sign. This was it, Old Parkers Road.

Time seemed to have stopped out here. Thickly leafed branches hung over the road from the oak trees. The road was littered with debris—branches, gravel, and acorns—that crunched under her tires.

An untamed pyramidal hedge blocked the view of a house from the road. *Lovely. No house markers.* The hedge opened briefly to expose a metal gate. Rust covered the surface of the gate, dripping orange down the sides of the curlicue scroll work.

How was she supposed to find Montgomery Manor? She read the directions again. *Look for the bargeboard and twin turrets.*

The hedge continued on the other side of the gate until it butted into the stone fence of the next property. This property's driveway was also closed off by a gate. Elise peered down the concrete path. Perched at the end was a three story mansion. The undergrowth had long ago claimed the driveway and the bushes and greenery now encroached the stairs and the pillars. Shutters bordered the upper balcony on the third floor. One shutter dangled haphazardly, as if the slightest wind would blow it off.

Forgotten by time.

She let her foot off the brake and edged forward. The next house lacked a gate, edged instead by a row of trees along the driveway line. The trees boughs dripped with Spanish moss and appeared black as they stretched towards the overcast sky.

At the end of the driveway stood another three-story house. This one with enormous white pillars, an expansive porch, and five brick chimneys. And there was the towers and white painted bargeboard. Her stomach cramped with nerves as she turned down the driveway.

She parked near the separate garage and walked up to the entrance. The house that seemed so full of splendor from the road showed its age and lack of care the closer she got. The pillars had appeared pure white in the distance, but up close were laced with a multitude of fissures running their lengths. Wide, white stairs led up to the front porch, stairs in dire need of paint and replacement of more than one rotting board. The porch itself was intact, with the exception of gray spiderwebs interspersed between the bargeboard that hung from the roof's edge.

The front windows were covered with curtains and didn't allow Elise a peek inside. Instead, only her own slender form was reflected back in the panes of glass.

Taking a deep breath, she knocked.

The door opened immediately.

A maid stood there, dressed as if she were auditioning for a play set in the early 1900's.

"Evening, mum," the maid spoke with a light accent. Her dark curls were pinned under a frilly cap.

Elise's eyebrows ratcheted up in surprise. *What in the world?*

"I'm here to see Myrtle Kennington," Elise said, even as her gaze scouted for what she could see behind the woman.

"Right this way." As the maid stepped back, her tight laced shoes squeaked against the parquet flooring.

Elise stepped inside expecting her shoes to squeak, too. She was relieved when they didn't.

The maid led Elise through the hall and down to the right. She stood in front of the parlor with her hand extended.

Elise walked in, filled with trepidation. A roaring fire lit the room, along with two Tiffany lamps. An old lady sat in a wing-back chair holding a fragile teacup in what appeared to be an equally fragile hand.

"Can I help you?" the woman asked.

Elise was further taken aback. *Didn't Lavina tell her I was coming?* "Hi. I'm Elise. I'm here to stay with you for a little bit."

The woman set down the teacup on its saucer and snatched up her cane. She stood shakily and tottered a few steps closer to Elise. "Who sent you?" the old lady scowled, her hand trembling as she held the cane.

Elise swallowed. "Lavina. Your niece."

"She sent you to protect me?" The old lady studied Elise from head to toe as she leaned on her cane. "Pshaw! You can't protect me from a squirrel trying to take my nuts."

"Well," Elise began in a soothing voice. "I'm here more as a companion until your other niece from Maine gets here. Just in case you need someone in the middle of the night."

"I don't need somebody to help me in the middle of the night. That's why I have Matilda. I need someone to protect me from the person who's moved back in."

"Somebody else has moved in?" *Was this the crazy Lavina had warned her about?*

Aunt Myrtle eyed her. "Somebody or something. Who knows in this house?" The old woman sidestepped around her like a crab scuttling for the water. "Lavina arranged it, I guess you're staying, then. You can call me Aunt Myrtle." The woman headed for the hallway, her cane thumping loudly. "Come, follow me."

"What a beautiful house you have here," Elise said as she looked around. The inside was even more extravagant than the outside, but again, in dusty disrepair. Back in the foyer, the crystal chandelier held none of its original sparkle. Instead, it glowed dully, coated with a layer of dust.

"I just don't know what Lavina Sue was thinking," Myrtle grumbled. "Hamilton!" she shrieked, startling Elise. It was surprising how much volume came from such a tiny woman. "Hamilton! Where are you?"

"Right here, ma'am." An old man seemed to materialize out of this air. His uniform had been stiffly pressed and his tie knotted smartly. A closer look showed shiny patches at his knees and a frayed cuff at his wrist. His white hair was slicked back, displaying a pink scalp at the crown.

"It appears we have a guest." Aunt Myrtle said crossly, then turning to Elise. "That is if you're planning to stay or are you just content to lollygag in my foyer?"

Elise grabbed her satchel more firmly. "Where would you like me to stay?"

Hamilton waved a glove in Elise's direction. "Right this way, ma'am."

"Top door to the left!" Aunt Myrtle directed, pounding her cane as emphasis.

"Yes, ma'am. The room you told us to tidy." The butler nodded to Myrtle and headed up the stairs. Elise followed.

There were two sweeping staircases, one that curved to the right, and one to the left. At first glance, the stairs appeared majestic, with its dark wood and white carved banister rails. But the gloss was gone up the center of the stair treads, worn away by countless feet trudging up and down.

The stairs creaked under her feet and showed years of dust in the crevasse between the railing and the tread. *I wonder why the maid or butler hasn't dusted the chandelier or vacuumed the edges on the steps?* Each step had a slight dip in the center from years of use. Sunlight peeked through the kite window and illuminated a cloud of dust motes. Elise walked up the stairs, feeling as though she wouldn't be at all surprised to see ghosts of years gone by trail down past her.

One step creaked especially hard under her foot, sounding like a shot from a gun. She jerked and clutched the railing.

"Mind your step, ma'am," Hamilton said in a monotone.

Up they went, around the bend and to the first landing. Elise eyed the large statue that greeted her.

Two ivory fairies stood together, one on a toadstool looking over the other's shoulder. The one on the toadstool held a giant blue globe that sparkled. The fairies' blind eyes stared straight ahead. At the base of their feet was a chip in the stone that extended a hairline fracture down to the base of the pedestal. A brown stain covered the edge of the chip.

Elise couldn't help the shiver that curled at the base of her spine. *Don't be silly. There's nothing strange about that. This house is old. The stain could have been there from years ago.*

But that brown looked an awful lot like old blood.

Elise looked up. Somehow the butler had lengthened the space between them by five or six steps. She stepped quickly after Hamilton.

He turned down the hall at the top of the steps. "Right this way, ma'am." His tone couldn't have been more bland if he was describing oatmeal. The second story floor was covered with a carpet, also threadbare down its center, that darkened to a ruby red along the edges of the wall. The wall was lined with family portraits. Her eye was drawn to the one in the middle, hanging crooked.

The doors were carved in a six cross pattern and all made out of the same heavy oak. Hamilton took her past four such doors before opening the fifth.

Elise paused in trepidation before straightening her shoulders and walking in.

The room was charming. Completely different from what Elise had expected. A pink chintz bedspread lay across the bed, looking fresh and clean. Both gabled windows were covered with matching chintz curtains and showed green glimpses of the estate's garden. There was even a small fire crackling in the fireplace.

"This is lovely," Elise said with a smile. She set down her bag. "Thank you so much."

The butler nodded. "Dinner is at six. Ms. Kennington is very prompt and expects everyone to be on time. Your washroom is just through these doors." He lifted a gloved hand to point to two doors at the side of the room. "And your closet is here. If you need any help unpacking, please use the phone's intercom and ask for Matilda." He pointed to the phone, an old white rotary dial. His face flushed with what looked like pride. "We've recently upgraded."

*Recent? He holds a new definition of the word recent.* "I appreciate it so much."

Hamilton turned to go.

"Excuse me! Before you go, I have a quick question for you."

The Butler blinked slowly and kept his hand on the door knob as if to cut off any long winded questions. "Yes, ma'am?"

"Have you noticed anything strange going on here?"

"No, ma'am. But, Ms. Kennington is quite lonely in these parts, since her children have moved away. I wouldn't be surprised if this wasn't some part of her plan to get them to return."

*That was a little rude of him to say.* Elise nodded. "Thank you again."

"Ma'am." With a nod, he shut the door.

Elise walked to the window and lifted the edge of the curtain. Far below was the rose garden, the flower heads dead and brown now. Elise frowned, wondering at the lack of care. Didn't Lavina say there was a live-in gardener? In the center was a giant hole with the dirt mounded to the side. Green hedges edged the rose garden like a living fence and marked out pathways through the estate.

The hedges were also not as maintained as they should have been, with odd branches that poked out from here and there.

Elise dropped the curtain and rubbed her fingers together, noting the lack of dust. This room had been cleaned thoroughly. *That frosty welcome was something else.* Elise thought about her friend and shook her head. *I'll bet Lavina didn't tell her Aunt that she'd passed the job to me. That girl owes me.*

She walked over to the dresser and pulled out a drawer. New liner paper had been laid that faintly smelled of lilac. She shuffled her few belongings from the satchel into the dresser and pushed the drawer closed.

*Time to freshen up.* She grabbed her purse and headed for the bathroom to wash her face.

Elise opened the bathroom door and froze. Filling her lungs to capacity, she let out a scream.

# Chapter 3

Elise's scream reverberated through the tiny bathroom. She screamed again.

Nothing. No one came running. She was alone.

Except she wasn't.

Hands shaking, legs quaking, she wobbled slowly toward the tub. The white lace shower curtain was partially closed. But not enough to hide the blue face of a man. Elise took a few more steps closer, hardly believing her eyes. Was he really dead?

He was dead alright. Fully clothed in a flannel shirt and blue jeans, he sat in six inches of water. And the knife sticking out of his chest was the exclamation mark.

Elise turned and ran from the bathroom. She flung open the door to the hallway. "Hamilton! Matilda! Somebody!"

Her words bounced around the hall. Not one answer. "Is anyone here? Help!" Elise ran out in the hall and clattered down the stairs. "Hamilton!"

The foyer was empty with no sound indicating that anyone was coming toward her. *There should be running. I'm screaming like a maniac! Where is everyone?* She hurried down the hallway that twisted left and right, passing arched oak entrances that led to a formal dining room, a study, a sitting room, the formal living room.

Elise poked her head inside each entrance in search for someone only to hurry to the next room. The heels of her shoes clattered like castanets against the wood flooring. "Hamilton! Aunt Myrtle! Matilda!"

"Mum?"

A nervous face poked out from a doorway at the end of the hall. Cheeks red like two turnips and curly hair escaping from under a mob cap. This was a new person to Elise.

"Oh, thank heavens." Elise scuttled toward her and into what turned out to be the kitchen.

The woman leaned back with alarm, her round body encased in a floury apron. "Mum? Can I help you?" The cook's eyes darted around behind Elise as if searching for someone to step in and rescue her from this crazed guest.

"I'm looking for Hamilton. Do you know where he is?"

Defeat flooded the cook's face at her inability to find someone else to take care of the situation. "Can I help, mum?"

"I seem to have... an unexpected person in my room." Elise stammered.

"Unexpected, mum?"

The blank look on the cook's face suddenly infuriated Elise. She straightened. "We need to find Hamilton immediately. And possibly Aunt Myrtle. We need to call the police."

The last word seemed to light a fire under the cook. She waddled around the room as if the butler might be hiding in one of the huge stew pots on the counter. Finally, eyes opening wide in triumph, she trundled to the phone on the wall. "I shall call him!"

She picked up the white phone and stared at the rotary dial while Elise took some deep breaths. Elise's hands trembled to snatch the phone away and call it herself. Slowly, the cook stuck her finger in the number and rotated the dial. Click. Click. Click. Click. The dial spun back to zero. She dialed another number.

Elise felt itchy watching, realizing she'd left her cell up in her room. *Hurry! Hurry! I need to call Lavina! And Brad!*

"Oh, hello?" the cook gave the receiver a flustered look. "Hello? Hamilton?" She shot a side-eyed glance at Elise before turning her back. "Come quickly to the kitchen," she whispered. "I have an issue." She drew out the last word in anxiety. "Okay? Okay." She clicked the phone back into the receiver and turned to Elise. Brushing her hands across the front of her rounded tummy, she announced, "He's on his way, mum."

Elise puffed a big exhale and tapped her fingers on her thigh. Just a few more minutes.

Footsteps hurrying along the passageway heralded the butler. He spun around the corner into the kitchen with his hair on top of his head raised in his rush. "Ma'am?" he asked, quickly smoothing his hand along the top of his shiny dome.

"Hamilton, you need to call the police. There is a dead man in my bathtub."

At Elise's proclamation the cook squeaked. Hamilton took a small step backward before regaining his professionalism. "After you, ma'am." He waved his hand for her to lead the way.

"I mean, right now. Call the police."

"I shall do it from your room, ma'am," Hamilton reassured her as he clasped his hands behind his back. "If there seems to be a need."

*A need? What in the world?* Inwardly, Elise seethed at being treated as though she were having the vapors.

The cook scurried after them. Hamilton raised an eyebrow but didn't impede her following.

The three of them took the stairs. Elise rushed ahead, only to slow down because of the stately pace the butler took. The poor cook was puffing by the time she reached the top of the stairwell. The three traveled down the hall. Once again, Elise noticed the portrait that hung crooked. *What's the matter with me? Good grief. What does it matter, now? There's a dead body up ahead!*

Elise opened the bedroom door and crossed the floor to stand outside the bathroom. Hamilton glanced in her direction before opening the bathroom door. Immediately, his lips tightened into two thin lines. Behind him, the cook gasped and covered her mouth.

"Cookie," Hamilton began. "Ring for the police."

The cook glanced about the room for the phone before sinking onto the bed. She covered her eyes as low sobs rolled through her. Her shoulders quaked.

Elise closed her eyes before grabbing her purse. "I have it," she told the Butler. Quickly, she dialed for the police. "Hello, I'd like to report a dead body. I just discovered it in my bathroom." At the request for the address, Elise passed the phone to Hamilton.

Hamilton's voice was sober as he relayed the address. "No, there won't be a need to try and resuscitate him. Yes, ma'am. It's undeniable that he is dead. His face is blue, ma'am. There is cutlery sticking out of his chest."

Cookie squealed again. Her fingers were white with the effort of clamping them across her mouth.

"Yes, I do recognize him, ma'am. He is our gardener."

# Chapter 4

The police arrived within fifteen minutes of the phone call, with Lavina hot on their tail. Elise nearly died to see the white Camaro screech in after the police cars, looking as if it were the one pulling the cops over.

Elise stood from the porch swing where she'd been waiting.

"Darlin', what have you done now?" Lavina exclaimed, getting out of her car. She waltzed up the stairs with the police, somehow pushing ahead of them. They eyed her in her tight blue dress and Louis Vuitton heels.

Matilda opened the front door. She wrung her hands in distress at the sight of the four police officers, only relaxing as Lavina approached.

"Where is Aunt Myrtle?" Lavina asked. The maid pointed to her right.

Lavina breezed down the hall in confident strides with Elise following behind, feeling like a puppy. *Darn those high heels. Hard to compete when one is wearing slippers.* The two women passed the butler on his way to greet the police.

Lavina gave Elise a cool glance. "Well, darlin', only a day here, and you've already discovered a dead body."

"Technically, that body was here before I was," Elise corrected. Lavina harrumphed and opened the parlor door.

Aunt Myrtle still sat in the same arm chair, the teacup sitting beside her. The fire had died down to red coals. Yarn piled high in a basket at her feet was slowly eaten away by her knitting needles. Glancing up from her work, she scowled at Lavina. "What are you doing here?"

"Hello, Auntie," Lavina said. She walked over and kissed her aunt's papery cheek. "I've heard you've had some excitement today, hmm?"

"Excitement." Myrtle took a sip of tea before her shaking hand returned it to the saucer on the table with a clack. "That darn gardener got himself offed. Typical of the outdoor paid help. Never dependable. And then Missy here," Myrtle's fingers with their overly large knuckles pointed in Elise's direction. "Had to go and call the coppers. And so here we are." Her gray eyes glanced toward the doorway. "And here they are."

"Ms. Kennington, I'm Officer Stone," began one of the policemen, this one appearing to be in his late fifties.

"Shouldn't you be removing your hats before you address me?" the old lady snapped.

The police man glanced at his partner, a mustached fellow who hid his grin behind a hand. Officer Stone lowered an eyebrow at his partner and cleared his throat in warning. It seemed to egg his partner on even more. With a sigh, Officer Stone removed his cap and held it over his chest. "As I was saying, Ms. Kennington, we've been called for a possible dead body. I've sent the other officers upstairs with the butler to assess the situation."

"There's no situation to assess. Rodgers, my gardener is dead. End of story."

Officer Stone opened his mouth when the speaker on his shoulder squawked. He pressed the mic. "Come in."

"That's a 187, captain."

"I'll call in the coroner." He looked back at the old lady. "Unfortunately, the story isn't as open and shut as you would like to believe, Ms. Kennington. The man is not only dead but undoubtedly murdered."

"Pshaw. Murdered in my house? You must be mistaken."

"He certainly didn't stab himself in the chest," Elise muttered to Lavina.

Lavina fluttered her eyes. "Stabbed? So crass."

Officer Stone glanced at Elise. "Are you the one that found him?"

Elise nodded, suddenly tense at the scrutiny from the officer. He pulled out his pad. "Let me just ask you a few questions."

Elise settled in the wing chair across from Aunt Myrtle. She had a feeling it was going to be more than just a few.

***

Several hours later, the coroner left with the body, everyone had been interviewed, and Elise's room had been thoroughly searched. The bedroom was currently cordoned off with yellow tape with Elise's battered valise sitting outside the doorway looking like an orphaned puppy.

The staff had been none too happy to relocate Elise into a new room, and the cleaning job had been hastily done. Elise looked around and tried to ignore the sinking dread inside her chest. The room was still dirty. "Lavina, maybe you need to call someone else."

"Someone else? Darlin, who am I going to call? It's just you and me here. How about if I stay with you tonight?"

"And how are you going to keep me safe?" Elise eyed her skeptically. "Throw a glass of wine in the killer's face?"

"You hush now. I have a few moves." Lavina settled on the bed before wrinkling her nose at the cloud of dust. "This has to go." She picked up the phone and rang for the house service. “Hamilton,” her voice was firm. “You need to immediately have both Matilda and Charlotte come up here and clean this room again. It’s disgraceful.” She hung up after his quick answer.

“See,” Lavina brushed her hands off and walked to the wing-back chair. “It’s getting better already.”

“Murder...,” Elise said again.

“Well, you heard the police. Their number one suspect is that transient the gardener hired as a helper this summer. He up and left, and without his last paycheck too. I’m sure that’s who did it.”

“Really, and why in my room?”

Lavina shrugged. “Maybe the transient lured him there after getting the knife. I have no idea. You really can’t explain why people do the things they do these days. Besides, you never know. Maybe that transient had been wandering the halls and stealing stuff all summer, and that’s who Aunt Myrtle heard.”

“So, she’s not so crazy after all.”

“Well, I wouldn’t go that far, but I guess I’ll have to pay better attention to what she says from now on.”

Pounding down the hall heralded Matilda and another maid, each with their arms loaded with bedding and cleaning supplies.

"This is Charlotte. Now, mum, if you don't mind moving to the parlor," began Matilda, her face flushed and sweaty. "I can clean this room lickety-split."

Charlotte was new to Elise, a young woman with eyes wide and innocent. She smiled at Elise and unwound the vacuum cleaner cord.

"Right," Elise said, "And, thank you."

The two housekeepers bobbed their heads as Lavina and Elise left the room.

In the hallway, Elise spied the crooked picture again. "You know, Lavina," she said as she reached for the frame. With a careful wiggle, she straightened the portrait. "You said this would be relaxing. Easy money, you said."

"Well, how can I help it that you have the worst luck in the world?" Lavina quipped back. She flipped her red hair off her shoulders. "Aunt Myrtle has the most sedentary life I know of. Until you came along that is."

"He was dead before I got here." Elise reminded. She shivered at the memory of the man's face. "Poor guy, I wonder why?"

Aunt Myrtle still sat before the fire in the parlor. "Back already?" she asked before patting her lap. A cat stretched from the other chair and blinked at the old lady. "Come here, you furry mouse trap. Come here and let me love you," Aunt Myrtle said crossly.

Despite the less than stellar invitation, the cat hopped down from the chair and meandered over to the old woman. He rubbed his cheek against her leg encased in thick, tan pantyhose while she continued to pat her lap. "Kitty! Up here, I said." The cat sprang into her lap, purring loudly. "So," Aunt Myrtle looked at Elise. "That was a one time deal, right? Not going to be calling the coppers again?"

Lavina cleared her throat. "Aunt Myrtle, it really wasn't her fault the police had to be called."

"I'm not talking to you. I'm talking to that girlie there. The cute one with the green eyes. Not the loud mouth that you are."

Lavina's face stiffened into a fake smile. She glanced at Elise. "Well, girlie?"

"There you go, being sassy again. I was just telling you to watch your P's and Q's a while ago."

"A long while, Aunt Myrtle. Like twenty years ago."

"Hush your mouth. It hasn't been that long." The old lady frowned and stroked the cat a little harder. The cat's ears flattened.

"I never planned to call the police, but find it hard to ignore the need in some circumstances. I really hope I won't be calling them anytime soon." *Unless another dead body sprouts out of this old house.* Elise smiled and tried to flash her most trustworthy look she could muster.

Aunt Myrtle's pale gray eyes studied her for a moment. "It's quite uncanny. You look just like her."

The old woman's stare unnerved Elise and she swallowed. "Look like who?"

"Her. You know, her."

Elise shook her head.

"Well, daggumit. I can't remember. All this commotion, can you blame me? Too much has happened today. Leave me alone, I'm tired." Aunt Myrtle pushed the cat off her lap and grabbed her cane. Without a backward look at either young women, she stumped out of the parlor and down the hall.

"Well," Elise began.

"That's Aunt Myrtle," Lavina finished.

Elise walked with Lavina back to the front door. "Now don't lie," Lavina took a deep breath. "I might be in a pinch, but I don't want to leave you. Are you sure you want to stay? This all is a bit much."

Elise opened the door and they both walked out onto the porch. She sighed. "Who else is going to do it? It really seems like now more than ever she needs someone here. I'll be fine. They have a suspect they're already searching for. The guy left his paycheck. I'm sure that means he's long gone."

Lavina closed her jacket tighter against the cold night air. Turning back, she raised an eyebrow. "I just want to know, what is it with you and dead bodies? Just bad luck?"

"Hey now, there weren't any on our cruise."

Lavina rolled her eyes. "You're getting stuck on semantics since you almost were one. But, then you always did do whatever you could to win an argument."

"We're not arguing. And I don't have bad luck."

"Maybe not, but I'd be buying a rabbit's foot if I were you. And stay away from any black cats."

A grinding *brrrr* of a motor-bike came from the entrance of the estate, sounding about as out of place in these plush quarters as a pig at a palace. Rounding the corner, under the maples, came the offending bike. Bent low over the handlebars was a little man dressed in biker gear, complete with old-fashioned aviator goggles.

"Who *is* that?" Elise asked.

Lavina turned to look. "That is Uncle Shorty."

"Uncle Shorty?"

"Well," Lavina pursed her lips in thought. "Not a real uncle. Not related to us at all, actually. His family has owned the estate next to Montgomery Manor for the last few generations. The families have always been each other's aunts and uncles. He's always been bugging Aunt Myrtle to sell because he wants to expand the property."

"Interesting." Elise nodded.

The old man came to a stop in front of the sweeping stairs, his bike backfiring just before he turned it off. He climbed down and slipped off his glasses, leaving red rings around his eyes.

Standing at just Elise's shoulders, he looked up with a cocky wink. His white hair stood out like a tumbleweed from the helmet but he didn't bother to smooth it down. Instead, he trudged up the stairs with confident thumps of his boots and knocked on the door.

It opened and he was quickly received by Hamilton.

"He's also Aunt Myrtle's very close friend." Lavina raised an eyebrow at Elise.

"You mean...?"

"Hush now. It's impolite to say more than that."

Elise was quite taken aback at the news that Aunt Myrtle possibly had a beau. Aunt Myrtle? She shook her head as Lavina climbed into the Camaro.

"Well, you keep in touch, you hear? Don't get into too much trouble." Lavina called from the window.

"Me?"

"Too much more trouble, I should amend." Lavina looked at Elise thoughtfully. "I'm serious. Don't make me worry any more than I already am."

"Relax. You're only a phone call away, and I have Brad if I need help." Elise shrugged toward the house. "And, apparently, Uncle Shorty, too."

A laugh shot out of Lavina. "You be good, now." She threw the car into reverse.

"You too!"

"Elise! Way to expect the impossible from me."

Elise smiled and waved goodbye. The car slowly backed out of the driveway, squealing the tires once Lavina was on the road.

# Chapter 5

Elise woke up late the next morning, having apparently slept through the breakfast bell. Trying to remember where she was, she blinked and looked around the room with the covers still pulled to her nose.

The memories from yesterday came crashing in.

Aunt Myrtle. Lavina. Police.

Dead man.

At the last thought, she groaned and pulled the covers over her head. *What have I gotten myself into?* She sighed and flung them back, causing her hair to snap with static electricity. Glancing at her watch, her eyes struggled to focus. *Crap! Max!* She jumped out of bed and ran for the bathroom.

Brad had already promised he'd let the cat in at night, but she needed to get there quickly and let him back out. Max had a strange aptitude to be vengeful, and she liked her couch legs whole and unmarred by the grooves of kitty anger.

After a little reluctance to even pull back the curtain, she finally took the quickest shower she could get away with before drying off and getting dressed. Her wet hair was slicked back, like seal's fur, into a bun. She felt cozy in her chunky pink sweater and jeans.

Elise left her room, gave the portrait a cursory look—*what the heck? Crooked again?*—before giving in and straightening it, and then bounded down the stairs. As she passed the fairy statue, she rubbed the globe for luck. For some reason the old house made her feel young, almost teenager-ish.

She kind of liked it.

Elise passed the dining room where Charlotte was just putting the finishing touches on a new table setting, presumably for lunch. Elise watched, curiously, as Charlotte walked around the table and touched the silver handle of each fork with a little murmur. At the last touch, the housekeeper stood back with a satisfied smile.

"Hello, Charlotte," Elise called out.

Charlotte whirled around with a squeal of surprise. "Oh, mum! You mustn't sneak up on a person like that." Her hands shook as she gripped the edge of the table.

"Oh, I'm sorry. I just came in." Elise checked her watch. "Is this for lunch?"

"Yes, mum. Breakfast was over two hours ago." Charlotte blushed. "My nerves get to me. It's been so quiet around here, with only Ms. Kennington dining since her children left."

"I can imagine so. Lavina told me she had two?"

"Yes. It's been awful lonesome for Miss Kennington since they left the country."

"When do you expect they'll be back?"

"I hardly know. Word is that they are establishing the Montgomery business in the foreign stock market. But then, what do I know about these things?"

The maid brushed the front of her apron and looked at Elise expectantly. "Will there be anything else, mum?"

"I have a weird question. Is Hamilton," Elise hesitated then, realizing how awful her question was going to sound, but now she was committed. "Is he as old as Aunt Myrtle?"

Charlotte giggled. "He's been around since she was first married. Which was, like, forever ago. He knew Ms. Kennington's father, Mr. Montgomery, before he passed."

"I was wondering. The chauffeur too?"

Charlotte nodded, her cheeks turning pink. "Yes. And the poor gardener too. Ms. Kennington is quite loyal to her staff. That makes this a dream job."

Elise was glad to see her smile. "You like working here, then?"

Charlotte's smile dropped just a bit, but she nodded again. "I do, mum. She pays me well and I've been saving my money."

"Really? Any big plans for it? Do you have a boyfriend?

The maid blushed and giggled. "I do. That's what I'm saving for. He's been offered a job out in California, and as soon as we can afford to, he says we'll get married and make a go of it down there."

"Oh! That's exciting! Does he live nearby?"

"You could say he does, but I'd rather not say where."

Elise nodded, not wanting to press too hard. She had one more question yet and she knew how cautious the staff was about outsiders snooping. "Your secret's safe with me. I won't tell. Hey, I've been just a tiny bit curious about one thing."

"Mum?" The word came out guarded.

"Well, when I drove up yesterday, I noticed at least four floors. But the stairwell seems to only go to three."

Charlotte's face relaxed. "Oh, you're correct. When the house was remodeled the fourth stairwell was taken down. Instead, there's a hidden hatchway that leads up there."

"Really? Now that's clever. Hidden away, you say? Did they use the extra space for something else?" Elise hoped the question would further draw Charlotte out. By the smile on the housekeeper's face, it looked as though it worked.

"Oh, yes, mum. I believe that space became the nook inside the laundry area now. It's quite helpful to be able to do the ironing in there rather than having to drag it down to the mudroom in the kitchen. Of course, that was way before my time."

"My goodness. That would have been difficult to haul the laundry down all those stairs."

"Oh, no, mum. Back then, they used the dumbwaiter. It's connected to the laundry room."

"Interesting. Is the dumbwaiter still in use?"

"I haven't seen it been put to use since I've been here. I imagine it's full of spiders and dust."

"Mm, you're probably right, especially in a house of this age. Is the hatch to the attic in the laundry room ceiling then?"

"No, mum." Charlotte shivered and rubbed her arms. "I wish! Actually, it's in my room and I detest it."

Elise noted Charlotte's strong reaction. "Why do you detest it? Does it send down cold drafts?"

"No, mum." Charlotte's gaze cut sideways toward the entrance before she continued, as if assuring herself they were alone. Her voice lowered. "I hear things."

Elise straightened and crossed her arms. "Hear things? At night? Oh, you poor thing. Like rodents?" She grimaced. "Yuck."

"It was only a rat, mum, if a rat were dragging a suitcase."

Elise's mouth dropped open before she quickly recovered. "Are you sure? Could it be a raccoon that somehow wiggled through the ox-eye? Did you see any evidence in your room that the hatch opening had been tampered with?"

"No one could have gone up there through the hatchway, mum. I'd been there all night. No, it was the ghost."

"The ghost?" Elise tried to keep her voice casual, ignoring the prickly sensation crawling up her arms.

"The one that haunts this place and steals our stuff."

Eyebrows raised, Elise continued. "You've had some of your stuff stolen?"

"Or moved around." Charlotte bit her bottom lip, looking uncertain at the direction the conversation was taking.

"Really! Like what?"

The housekeeper cleared her throat and fidgeted with a thread hanging off one of her cuffs. "Just some small things. It won't seem much to someone like you."

"I'd love to know all the same."

"Well, there was my toothbrush."

"Your toothbrush was moved?"

Charlotte blushed. "I know that sounds silly, but I like it in a certain place, facing a certain way"

Elise nodded, suddenly remembering the way Charlotte had checked the door the night before, touching the knob three times. It had happened just now as Charlotte had touched each fork in its setting. It seemed the maid had a bit of an obsessive compulsive disorder. “Okay, I get it. And it was moved?”

“Yes,” Charlotte pulled her sleeves down before giving a resigned sigh. “The bristles were facing the wrong way.” She lifted her head as if daring Elise to say anything more.

“Wow, that's weird. And it couldn't have fallen? Joggled in the container?” Elise continued in spite of Charlotte's vigorous head moving in denial.

“You don't believe me?” she said, her face looking defensive.

“I believe you. Definitely.” Elise knew the toothbrush had moved, but really by someone?

“It's that ghost trying to mess with me. In all honesty, I'd leave this job if I could. I don't want to deal with any ghosties. But, I'm saving my money, so....”

Elise nodded. “Why do you think a ghost would want to mess with you?”

“Why does it want to mess with any of us?” Charlotte winked an eye. “Just ask Miss Myrtle.”

“Are you saying...?”

“Miss Myrtle knows the ghost personally. And now, if there's nothing else, I really need to get back to work.”

Elise frowned, thinking about the last comment about Aunt Myrtle knowing the ghost. “No, that's all. I'm sorry to keep you, Charlotte.”

The housekeeper bobbed her head and left the room.

# Chapter 6

After dinner that night, Elise joined Aunt Myrtle once more in the parlor. It seemed to be the start of their new nightly routine together.

"I know who you look like." Aunt Myrtle said before making kissy noises to the cat. Her kisses sounded more like the sucking to keep her dentures in her mouth.

"You do?" Elise answered, mildly jealous as she watched the cat stretch and stalk over to his owner. *I miss Max, that little rogue.* Max had given her the silent treatment that morning when she opened him his can of wet cat food and let him out for the day. Not even a little piece of lunch meat would lure him over. In a panicked phone call to Brad, he'd assured her that Max was still friendly at night when he'd let the cat back in.

"That's right, I do," Aunt Myrtle continued, pulling Elise from her musings. "Your great, great grandma."

Elise's mouth dropped open. *This must be it. This the crazy Lavina warned me about.* "My...."

"What? Have you cloth for ears? That's right. Your great, great grandma. ." Aunt Myrtle blew on her tea and regarded Elise through the steam over the top of the cup. "It's come full circle with you here to be my companion again."

"I'm kind of in shock. I've never heard anything about this. Are you saying that my great, great grandma used to live here?"

Aunt Myrtle nodded. "She did. Papa hired her to watch over me. I was always such a handful. Never would settle down and have that big coming-of-age ball that Mother had wanted."

"Oh. Why not? A ball sounds like fun."

Aunt Myrtle grimaced. "A bunch of filly-fally with girls primping and making goo-goo eyes at the young men. I never could hold to them. I met Mr. Kennington on a trip to New York City. Oh, I fancied myself a flapper back in those days. Had the short hair. Drew the line down the back of my legs to imitate stockings." Aunt Myrtle grinned. "Of course, Papa was mortified since we could afford those little self-indulgences, but he didn't realize that real stockings wouldn't have been the bees' knees."

Elise settled back in the chair and smiled. "You sound like you had a luxurious young adulthood."

"The lap of luxury." Aunt Myrtle stroked the cat, who had closed his eyes in a cat smile. "I suppose some would have called it that. We certainly weren't hurting for money, that's for sure. Papa had always been frugal, squirreling money away for as long as I could remember. All of this," she waved her hand in the air to indicate the house, "is supported just on the interest of his investments alone. Even the Depression didn't hurt us too badly. After the war ended, Papa bought up every Freedom Dollar he could find. He was just tickled to death by them. Then, he started the Montgomery Loan Institute, dedicated to helping families get back on their feet after the Great Depression."

"Wow. That's really incredible."

"That was him all right. That's the perfect word. He was incredible." Aunt Myrtle stroked the cat's head again, looking lost in thought. The clock ticked in the background, highlighted by the silence.

Elise didn't mind the quiet. She stared into the flames dancing on the hearth and relished the heat baking her face and fronts of her legs.

"I'm going to bed." Aunt Myrtle said abruptly.

Her words startled Elise, who slowly stood up in response. *Time for bed, I guess. After all, Aunt Myrtle runs the show.* "Okay. I guess I'll head there too. Sleep well, Aunt Myrtle."

"I'll sleep how I sleep. And, if you want to sleep well, I suggest you ignore any weird noises."

"Noises?"

"Every night I hear them. Little feet." Aunt Myrtle patted the head of the cat. Pat. Pat. Pat. The cat didn't seem to appreciate the demonstration of the feet on his head.

Elise forced her face to remain expressionless. "Oh. Okay, then. Thank you and I'll see you in the morning."

"Not if I see you first!" The old lady cackled.

***

Once in her room, Elise discovered she really was tired. Her nightly routine took just a few minutes before she headed to bed, bringing her phone with her. Bored, she scrolled through Pinterest until the screen blurred through sleepy eyes.

Tap. Tap. Tap.

*Oh, come on. Is Aunt Myrtle playing a joke on me?* She lifted her head off the pillow to listen. There it was again. Tap. Tap. Tap. A cold flush ran down Elise's neck. She knew exactly what that sound was; high heeled shoes. Aunt Myrtle's voice rang through her head. *"Every night, I hear them."*

Elise pulled the covers up around her neck and took a deep breath to calm herself. *Okay, chill out. It's probably....* Her memory ran through the women that lived there. Cookie? Matilda? Charlotte? Aunt Myrtle? She glanced at her watch and shivered again. Two am.

Clack. Clack. Clack. The heels tapped on the floor. *How far away were they? Maybe the room next door?* Elise scrambled from the bed and reached for her cardigan hanging on the back of a chair. She buttoned it up and grabbed her cell, shoving it into one of the pockets. After a few moments of searching, she found her sneakers and tied them on.

*Am I really doing this?*

*Yep. I really am.*

She slid out the phone and hovered over Brad's number, ready to press it at any second. Quietly, she tiptoed to the bedroom door and opened it. Her spine stiffened at the squeak the door made as it swung back on its hinges.

She paused and listened again.

Nothing.

Which room were the footsteps coming from? The one right next door to her or the one across and down the hall? She hemmed and hawed for a second before she headed for the adjacent room. Her heart rate amped up with each step she took.

Elise reached for the handle and turned, trying to be as sneaky as possible. At the last second, she flung it open and reached for the light switch.

*Crap.* There was no light switch. With a flick, she changed her phone to the flashlight and swept the light around the room.

Empty.

She hurried over to the porcelain flower lamp on the other side of the room and clicked it on.

Empty alright. The room looked as if no one had been in it for years. Decades even. Dust covers shrouded the bed and chairs, leaving them with the appearance of curled-over goblins. The fireplace grate was empty of even the barest sign of ashes. Elise rubbed her fingers together, feeling the grime from the brief contact with the lamp.

Something dropped behind her. Elise swiveled, and her heel caught on the corner of a wrinkle in the rug. She tripped forward into the dresser to catch her fall as the cell phone flew from her hand. Her hands shook as she tried to steady herself against the dresser. *So much for stealth and surprise.*

With a deep breath, she scanned the floor for her phone, locating it a few feet away near the wall. As she scooped it up, she noted a strip of wall paper had pulled away and was curling upwards.

She stood, with a resigned feeling, and flipped off the light. The trip had drained her adrenaline and now she moved forward almost woodenly. It was quiet in the hall as she marched for the other room.

With no fanfare, she swung the next room's door open.

Dark. Quiet. An exact replica of the other room. Moonlight sifted through the crack between the curtains and kept the room from being pitch black. She swung the beam of the cell's flashlight from corner to corner. The light bounced off a similarly clothed bed and chair. Another empty fireplace.

But wait. What was that? There in the corner? Some piece of strange furniture.

Still on tiptoes, Elise walked over to an identical lamp and flipped it on, illuminating the room. A scurrying sound came from under the bed. Elise froze. Something was under the there. She listened, wondering if she should run. There was another bump and then a sharp squeak.

A rodent. Most likely a rat.

Elise shivered, both in relief and in horror. She hated rats. But, how had the rat made the tapping noise? Chewing on something?

*I don't know, but I'm not bending down to find out.*

She walked over to the covered shape that stood tall in the corner. Cautiously, she reached for the dust cover.

Warnings buzzed in her head—*don't touch it. It's not yours*—but she whisked it off anyway.

The cloth threw up a cloud of dust as it fluttered to the floor. She coughed and waved her hand.

Blinking, she looked at the object.

A Victorian dollhouse sat on a small armoire. She felt a bubble of childish delight as she leaned forward to examine it. Four stories tall, the house was complete with two towers. Tipping her head, she could see there was even a wrap-around veranda. Oddly familiar.

She leaned closer to peek inside. The bottom floor was an overlay of miniature brown parquet flooring with two twin staircases winding up the side of the room.

Elise sucked in her breath. The house was a replica of Aunt Myrtle's. Hurriedly, she looked for confirmation. There was the passageway to the kitchen. There was the parlor where the police had come to talk to Aunt Myrtle last night.

She leaned in further. *Oh my heavens!* There was the fairy statue on the landing. There was her own bedroom! And here was the very room she stood in now.

Her mouth dropped open at the intricate detail. She stooped to study the kitchen again. There was even a miniature cook standing before counters that were covered with various baking ingredients and miniature pies. Cheese and onions hung from the tiny pantry ceiling. The living room had a grand piano. Elise couldn't resist the temptation and touched one of the tiny keys. A thrill ran down her spine at the tiny note it emitted.

The dining room held replicas of a man and woman sitting with minuscule teacups in their hands. A stack of pretend toast sat on a plate between them. Miniature place settings were arranged before them, and the tiny plates even held crumbs.

She followed the hallway back to the foyer, her eyes taking in the chandelier and art sculptures. On the second floor, she was delighted to see miniatures of the very portraits she walked by every day.

The room she was standing in now was perfectly replicated in nearly every detail. At the desk, a miniature girl with blonde braids sat with a pen in her hand. A red damask quilt covered the bed. Curiously, Elise walked over to the bed and turned up the edge of the dust cloth. She smiled when a red duvet peeped out from under it.

She examined the dollhouse again. The room she'd been given was slightly different. Most notably, the bed was covered with a blue and white pin-striped quilt. A girl doll—this one with brown curls—lay on the bed with a book in her hands, legs crossed. The window coverings were also revised to match the bedspread. There was another significant change. In the corner was the dollhouse on its stand.

*Wow. It had originally been in my room.*

Elise stood on her toes to peep into the third story. More bedrooms, what looked like servant's quarters. The most upper-level held an attic filled with miniature discarded items. There was a wooden rocking horse, a sewing mannequin, and a few scattered trunks.

She started to settle back from her toes when something else in the house caught her attention. A portion of the attic had been walled off into one more room. A tiny bedroom.

Grabbing the armoire for balance, she tried to see the details of the room. She flashed the light of the phone inside. It was plain, just a little bed, a dresser, and an old fashioned wash basin.

*Interesting.*

She relaxed back off of her toes and bit the inside of her lip. *Very interesting.*

Elise glanced around the bedroom again but, besides the shrouds, everything seemed in order. Nodding, she walked to the lamp, snapped it off and used the cell's flashlight to see her way out.

*Let me just check something.* She passed her room and headed for the original room she'd been given. Pausing, she looked up and down the hall to be sure no one was coming. Even at two in the morning, she felt the need to be cautious. Then she ducked under the yellow tape and entered.

Moonlight sifted through the crack between the curtains and kept the room from being pitch black. Using her cell, she maneuvered over to the lamp and turned it on.

She glanced around the room, checking to see if anything had changed, before moving to the far corner. Bending low, she swept the light over the floor. Discoloration showed a rectangle in the floorboards. That's where the armoire used to sit. She stood and examined the wall. The wallpaper here in this corner was darker, most likely hidden away from the sun for years.

She studied the floor again. A scrape in the wood led away from the discoloration. She squatted and touched it. It was fresh and deeply dug through the layers of stain and lacquer.

*Obviously, the dollhouse had been here for years. Elise thought about the blonde little girl in the room. Maybe for as long as when there were little girls in the house. Did one of those girls represent Myrtle? Someone else?*

Frowning, she clicked off the light and shut the door. *Why would they have moved it in here? Is it because they thought I'd be sleeping in that room?*

Deep in thought, she walked down the line of portraits. The one she'd fixed was crooked again, a portrait of a man. But that wasn't what stopped her cold.

The portrait next to it was missing.

# Chapter 7

Astonished, Elise stared at the wall. *What the heck is going on here? That portrait was there tonight. I know it was. I would have definitely noticed it missing.* Elise remembered how much the crooked picture had bothered her. There's no way she wouldn't have noticed a missing one. She held the cell's light up to the wallpaper, showing a darker rectangular patch on the wallpaper that outlined the missing portrait, just like the darker patch in the other room.

Her brow furrowed as she flashed the light down both ends of the hall. Of course no one was there. Puzzled, she returned to her room and shut the bedroom door. She locked it and leaned against the solid wood.

The fire cracked and spit a spark out on the hearth, causing her to jerk at the noise. She walked over and reached for the metal poker. After stirring the coals, she grabbed a log from the pile someone had left—probably Charlotte or Matilda—and fed the flames. A stray branch on the bark, that somehow had missed the ax, caught fire first and the pine needles snapped, filling the room with a woodsy scent. She breathed in, with her hands out to the fire. Somehow, the excursion to the other bedrooms had chilled her to the bones. After a minute of rubbing her arms, she crawled back into bed.

Elise plumped up the pillow under her head and stared up at the ceiling. Was that the noise that Aunt Myrtle had heard? Just a few rats? And, why had the dollhouse been moved? It looked like it would take several men to move it along with that great armoire. Where was the portrait? Did it have anything to do with the dead gardener?

She punched the pillow and rolled to her side, eyes wide open in the dark. *I can't wait to ask Aunt Myrtle about the dollhouse in the morning*. Her nose wrinkled as she imagined how she'd have to try and explain it. There was just no way not to make it sound like she'd been snooping. *But honestly, Aunt Myrtle will understand me investigating a noise.* She pulled up her phone and scrolled through the messages, wishing one was from Brad. She'd love to talk with him right now. But not at 2:30. No, definitely not.

Brad's face swam in her memory, making her smile. He was such an amazing bonus she'd gotten from moving back to her home town after her divorce. Years ago they'd gone to high school together and had been reacquainted when Lavina had been dragged into a murder mystery.

He was such a good guy too, watching Max for her while she was out here at the Manor. They'd made plans to explore Highjack Ridge in a couple days, a six-mile hike with an expansive overlook of Angel Lake that the town was legendary for. She'd only been to the top once when she was seven, riding the last little bit of the trail on her dad's shoulders. She remembered shivering with excitement on the way down as her dad had run along the trail.

She was even more excited to go explore it with Brad.

Ever since she'd gotten back from her cruise, Brad had been busy with police work. He was actually leaving soon for a week to do training at the academy. This would be the first time they'd gotten to spend time together in a while.

She couldn't wait. Because emails and messages just weren't cutting it anymore.

❊❊❊

The next morning, Elise woke after a fitful night's sleep. She rolled over in bed and stared out the window. The gauzy curtain blurred her view but she could make out the trees blowing hard outside.

Stormy weather. Lovely.

With a sigh, she sat up in bed and rubbed her eyes, then trudged over to the bathroom. The tub's faucet protested loudly as she turned the handle and spurted out a bellow of orange water before finally running clear. She flipped the lever for the shower and climbed in. It took forever to muster up the tiniest bit of lather with the shampoo. Finally, she gave up and rinsed her hair.

Elise dried herself in a towel that wafted the scent of lavender. She held it to her nose and sniffed, then hung it over the shower rail. Naked, she wandered back into her room where she found her jeans and t-shirt and dressed. Then she yanked up the blankets into a sort-of-made bed and glanced at her watch.

Thirty minutes until breakfast. Time enough to explore.

Crouching down, she fished her shoes from under the bed, laced them up, and left her room as quietly as possible.

It was silent on the second floor, but noise drifted up from the downstairs. Comforting sounds, like a woman humming and the clang of a pot from the direction of the kitchen.

Elise glanced at the hallway wall. The blank spot seemed to scream the absence of the portrait. *This is going to drive me crazy. Who took it down?*

She remembered adjusting the crooked one next to it, but couldn't remember who the missing portrait had been of. She studied the other pictures. The first one was an elegant lady who sat in a chair with a tea cup in her hand. The next one was a Cocker Spaniel with sad eyes. Here two little girls rested on a blanket in the shade of a tree with various toys around them. The next showed a man in a suit behind a woman. This one was of a man alone, the man graying and in a hunter's cap. The collection seemed like a complete family. Who could be missing?

*I wonder if the dollhouse would tell me.* With a glance to be sure she was alone, she headed down to the bedroom with the dollhouse. *Watch. This is about the time that somebody will show up and bust me.*

Prickles formed on her neck as she opened the door to the room and quickly shut it behind her. Turning around, she was surprised that the room was not any cheerier by the morning light. In fact, it looked straight out of a funeral house, with the way the furniture was covered in black dust covers. *The only thing missing is the casket. Heck, we even had a body.* Ignoring the chill that visual brought, she walked to the dollhouse.

Last night, she'd noticed how amazingly accurate the miniature house had mirrored Montgomery Manor, so she fully expected to see the tiny hallway filled with portraits.

Finding it, she gasped out loud.

Right in the middle of the lineup was a blank space, the very same portrait that was missing in the hall.

*What in the world is going on here?*

Her hands traced through her hair as she straightened up, her brain spinning a million miles a minute. *Okay. What have I gotten myself into? Cuckoo-ville here.*

*Was the miniature picture missing last night? Was I just so overwhelmed with everything that had happened that I didn't notice either one was gone?* She glanced around the room. Everything seemed to be untouched. There were no mysterious footprints anywhere, no smudgy fingerprints. She walked to the window and tried it. The latch was secure. Same with the other window.

Whoever had taken the portrait had come through the house.

But what was the point? Why take a painting and then the miniature replica also? It didn't make any sense.

The house bell dinged, announcing breakfast. Shaking her head with confusion, Elise left the bedroom, this time making double sure the door was shut firmly behind her.

She took the stairs solemnly. The third step surprised her again when it gave a gun-like crack under her foot.

Downstairs in the dining room, Aunt Myrtle sat primly at the head of the table. A small egg cup and a plate of toast before her. She didn't look up as Elise entered, making Elise feel on guard.

"Hello, Aunt Myrtle," Elise walked over to where a place had been set for her.

"You're late." She sounded offended as she spoke sharply.

Elise looked down at her lap. *This explanation needs to be good.* "I'm so sorry. Actually, I stopped to study the paintings in the hallway. They're pretty amazing. All of your family?" She stirred cream into her coffee and watched the white swirl across the black, wondering if she could continue. Would it upset the elderly woman? *I have to know.* "Aunt Myrtle, I couldn't help but notice that one of the portraits was missing from the hallway."

Aunt Myrtle didn't miss a beat. "That was Anna." She took a sip of tea and rested the cup back in the saucer with aged-shaking hands. Elise ignored the rattle of the china.

"Anna? Who's Anna?" Elise asked.

"My sister." The old woman picked up her spoon. She pulled her china egg cup with its painted yellow daisy closer and slowly scooped out the top of the egg. The spoon quivered between her fingers.

"Oh? I haven't met her yet."

Aunt Myrtle's eyes lit up as she glanced at Elise. "I'd have been surprised if you'd said you did. She's been dead these last sixty years."

Elise choked on her coffee. She snatched the cloth napkin from her lap and held it over her mouth as she coughed into it.

Aunt Myrtle watched her with amusement. "You okay? Catch a house-fly?"

Feeling red-faced, Elise waved her off, still trying to catch her breath. She took a sip from her water glass. "I'm fine. Sorry. You caught me off guard there."

"Oh, you didn't know about my sister?" Aunt Myrtle calmly continued. "I thought for sure Lavina Sue would have told you. There was a large gap between the two of us. Six years. She was a proper young lady while I was still a tomboy. Mother always said I was the apple of Papa's eye." Aunt Myrtle's finger rested against her bottom lip as she looked outside. The light from the dining room windows caused her pale gray irises to nearly blend in with the whites of her eyes. "And Anna was hers."

Aunt Myrtle blinked a few times and sighed. Turning back, she poured herself another cup of tea with an unsteady hand.

"How old were you when she died?" Elise gently asked.

"Eight years old. Old enough to know what happened."

"What.... What did happen, if I can ask?"

"What does it matter? Dead is dead, in the end. Mother said it was my fault. Everything and everyone was in such a commotion. People avoided me for days after."

*Her fault?* Sorrow gripped Elise at the thought of an eight-year-old crying alone in the corner. "Your Papa didn't tell you different?"

Aunt Myrtle's bottom lip quivered and she quickly licked it. "Ahh, Papa." She paused, staring into her tea. Her hand smoothed down the arm of the chair before dropping into her lap and she tipped her head. "He was such a dear. Such a bear of a man. Yes, he came and found me and held me. But things like that weren't spoken about in those days. That's not how things were done."

Aunt Myrtle paused to take another bite of egg, and maybe to collect herself. After a moment, she continued. "He left that sort of thing to your great, great grandma. Life was very different after Anna died." She placed the spoon down with a chatter on the plate. "But now she's back."

The old lady's words were like cold fingers running down Elise's spine. "You think Anna's here?"

"She comes from time to time. Has for years."

"How do you know it's her?"

"She makes her presence known. Her bed will be slept in, things moved around."

"I actually was in her room last night. I thought I heard something." Despite everything, Elise felt heat rise in her cheeks. "I think it may have been a mouse. I, uh, I saw a dollhouse in there."

"Ah. The dollhouse was mine, but Anna always wanted it."

"Did it used to be in your room? I saw a spot on the floor."

"Yes. The room I grew up in." The old woman squeezed her hands together before giving Elise a shaky look. "That is before Anna moved the house into hers a few months back."

Elise jerked in her seat. "She's the one that moved it?"

Aunt Myrtle's eyes narrowed at Elise. "Now, don't you go thinking I'm loony tunes. I heard her the other night. Clack Clack Clack!" Aunt Myrtle's fingers walked down the arm of her chair. "Her high heels."

"She wears high heels?"

"She wears whatever she wants. Are you going to be the one to tell her no?"

Elise shook her head, wondering how in the world she got herself into this conversation.

Aunt Myrtle smiled with satisfaction. "That's what I thought. Specters tend to make their own rules." She pulled her glasses up by a tangled chain that hung around her neck and situated them on her nose. Her eyes glittered behind the lenses when she turned to Elise. "But what's an old lady like me know, anyway?"

# Chapter 8

After breakfast, Elise left the dining room and wandered through the hall toward the formal living room. Aunt Myrtle had said she would be gone for the day at a ladies' luncheon. Something about Cribbage Club.

Elise had only glanced into the living room briefly on her first day here, but she remembered a pair of French doors. Although it was dark and broody outside, it wasn't raining yet and those doors were the simplest way she could think of to get outside to the garden.

Elise tugged her cell phone free from her pocket and typed. **Can't wait for our hike! Feel like visiting me here? I can show you around.**

Brad immediately texted back. **I think Max gave me a sore throat**

Elise frowned. *Great. Using Max now? Does Brad really have a sore throat or is he avoiding me?* She sighed and texted back. **That darn cat. Feel better soon!** *This is the reason why women stay single and become cat ladies.*

The entrance of the living room was marked with a giant vase of Calla Lilies that sat on a pedestal. Their heavenly scent filled the air, and she stopped to admire them. Humming alerted her that someone else was in the room. She looked around to see Matilda with a duster.

"Good morning, Matilda. How're you doing this morning?"

"Very good, mum. And you?"

"I'm doing great." Elise hesitated for a moment before forging ahead. "Actually, I didn't sleep too well last night. I guess this place has a few critters living in it?"

"Critters?" Matilda's face was drawn and tense. She paused with the duster and waited.

"Yeah," Elise walked over to the French doors and looked outside. Leaves lay in muddy dark clumps on the patio. "A mouse, I think? Have you seen any rodents here?"

"Well, bless your heart. Scared of a mouse? They're fairly common in these parts." The duster moved briskly again. "In a house this old, you're bound to have a few four-legged inhabitants."

"I guess that's true, but all the same, they're not my favorite. Especially when I hear them moving around late at night. And after, you know...the gardener."

Matilda nodded with a sympathetic look. "Oh, yes. Yes, I quite understand."

"Life's been pretty crazy around here this last week, huh?"

"Oh, mum, you can't even believe the things I've seen here lately."

That piqued Elise's curiosity. "Like what, Matilda?"

The duster froze over a clock on the wide fireplace mantle. Matilda licked her lips and looked over her shoulder as if she expected someone to be there. Seeing no one, she beckoned to Elise to come closer.

"I'm not one for gossip and I'm not blithering about fairy tales but," here her voice dropped several octaves and the housekeeper leaned closer. "Someone's been moving things around here."

"Moving?"

"Aye!" The housekeeper's eyes widened and she quickly cupped her hand around her mouth to whisper, "And they took my shoes."

Elise was flabbergasted. "They took your shoes?"

The housekeeper nodded. "Quite a few days later, they put them back, but my shoes haven't been right since. These 'uns are smaller than the other pair."

Elise glanced down at the housekeeper's feet shod in sensible brown, laced shoes. "Are these...?"

"Nah. These aren't them. These are my work shoes. They nicked my Sunday best."

"And put them back." Elise raised her eyebrows.

"That's right, but they give me awful calluses now." Matilda bent down to illustrate. "Right here, on these last two toes."

Elise nodded, feeling a little unsure. Was this just an example of a fantastic imagination from a bored housekeeper? Who would steal a pair of shoes only to replace them with the wrong size? "I'm sorry about that. Has anything else happened like that?"

"Oh, there's more, there's lots more."

Elise had taken a step towards the French doors and paused. She looked questioningly at Matilda.

"They took my eggs too," the maid continued.

Feeling incredulous, Elise sucked in a breath. *Was everyone loony in this place?* "Your eggs?" Now, this couldn't be true.

"Aye."

"Did they put those back too?"

Two lines deepened between Matilda's eyebrows. "What are you, daft?" A shocked look washed over the maid's face. "I mean, sorry mum. I spoke out of turn." She began to dust again, mumbling, "But, how could eggs return?"

"Well, where were they?"

"On a plate mum, with a side of ketchup." Matilda turned her back in a dismissive way, flipping her duster about. She clearly was disgusted with Elise's frivolity.

"From the... kitchen?"

"Yes, mum. Where the likes of us eat our breakfast." Matilda glanced back and, seeing the concern on Elise's face, seemed to decide to open up some more. "I only left my plate for a moment, see. And when I came back they were gone." The maid frowned. "That was a Sunday morning too. Calluses and no eggs. Not a good day. No, mum. Not a good day."

Elise nodded thoughtfully. She continued to the door and opened it. "Well, thank you for sharing, Matilda. If you can think of anything more, please come find me."

"I will mum. I'm watching." The housekeeper's rounded eyes roved back and forth. "I'm always watching."

Nodding again as if reassured, Elise hurried out the door and into the garden. She zipped her hoodie tight. The air held a threat of warning of the coming storm with its cold bite. Under her feet, the grass was thick and spongy with moss. She looked behind her and saw a trail of her footsteps. Around her, a breeze stirred the branches in the fruit trees making their branches rasp. She shivered and dug her hands into the hoodie's pockets.

Looking about, she took in the expansive garden and headed toward the maze in the center of the yard.

The maze was made of green hedges. They towered overhead, their raggedy tops having long overgrown the trimmed box shape. The grass gave way to dirt as the path entered the maze.

A balding bush marked the entrance and she walked into the maze feeling confident. She'd learned the secret long ago when she and Lavina used to do the corn maze every October. If they got lost, they stayed to the left at every turn. Eventually, it will lead to the exit.

The only thing different about this maze from the corn maze was that there was no way through if you made a mistake. The bushes were thick and impenetrable. If she got lost, she'd be stuck doing the left-turn trick.

The maze hadn't looked that complicated from her window, and she headed in the direction she remembered the center rose garden being. The sky overhead had become darker with more clouds, making the light in the maze even gloomier. She walked quickly.

It was an easy maze and in only eight or ten turns she'd made it to the center. Elise looked around, disappointed. From her window, she'd seen the decay, but she'd held out hope that some would still be in bloom.

She walked over to the dirt pile and hole at the center of the garden and peered inside. The bottom was nothing but a muddy puddle. Glancing around, she tried to find the reason it had been dug but saw nothing.

White benches covered in fallen leaves sat on the outskirts of the garden. She walked over to one and climbed up to look for the Manor.

There it was, appearing every bit as miniature in the distance as the toy one in the house. She searched for her room and thought she'd located it as the one with the curtains drawn open.

With a deep sigh, she clambered down and sat. It was peaceful in here and not nearly as windy. Almost like a private, little shelter from the world.

She was just about to entertain some fanciful thoughts from one of her favorite childhood books when she heard a noise.

*What in the—* There it was again. A cough. Her blood froze in her veins as she realized someone was in the maze with her. She stood, her head swiveling in the cough's direction. She looked at the exits, all four of them that opened into the rose garden. *Which one did I come from?* She took a step towards the closest one, feeling turned around as to how to get out. Closing her eyes for a moment, she pictured the view of the maze from her bedroom. She gritted her teeth. It was useless.

There was the cough again, softer this time, but igniting her to move. She had to make a choice and try to find her way back. What if it was that transient again? *All right. Can't stay here.*

The wind picked up and caused the tops of the hedge to sway. *Lovely, I can just see being caught out here in the rain. With a strange man. Even better.* Her sarcasm drove a muffled snort out of her.

Quickly, she moved away from the direction of the cough and retraced her trail. Left, go left every time. This rule should have worked, which is why finding the dead end in front of her left her flabbergasted. *How could this happen? I went right every time before.* Had she? What about that weird Y?

Adrenaline gave a tiny warning squeeze which she blew away with a deep breath. *I'm okay. This isn't that big of a maze. I'll figure it out.*

Another cough and this one sounded closer.

*Who on earth is that? It's not the gardener.*

She shivered. *Because the gardener is in the morgue.*

A vision of a toe-tag caused the panic she'd been fighting to blossom in her chest. *And I don't want to be the next one.* She hurried around the next corner, her feet scuffling through the leaves, no longer concerned if she was quiet. *Just get me out. Get me out of here.*

Her chest tightened at the next T and she looked left and right. Everything appeared the same. How did she get her? *Keep going left. Just go left again.*

Taking the left, she ran down the corridor and then turned left again. *I have to be getting close. There weren't that many turns.* Up ahead was the balding brush. Relief flooded her as she tore down the aisle towards the exit of the maze.

A man clad in a black raincoat stepped out, blocking the exit. Elise stifled a scream at the sight of him.

"Are you okay, ma'am?" he asked. The wind picked up and he reached for the hood of his raincoat and tugged it lower over his face.

Still taking a tentative step towards the exit, she nodded. "I wasn't expecting to see anyone."

She caught a glimpse of man's mouth as he smiled. His hand remained jammed in his coat pocket and seemed to be gripping something. "You should head inside. Lucky you found your way out before the storm." He glanced up at the gray sky.

"Thank you. And you are…?"

"Charles. I help out the gardener from time to time."

Elise gave a quick nod. "Well, it's nice to meet you, Charles. I'll see you around." She stepped around him and made a hasty retreat through the exit.

Once outside the garden, her chest heaved. She ran half-way across the lawn before she leaned over and rested her hands against her knees, trying to catch her breath.

With another look at the sky, she hurried inside the dining room and firmly closed the French doors behind her. Heart hammering, she lifted the edge of the curtain and stared out at the pyramidal hedge. Where was he? Had he followed her out?

A feminine throat clearing had Elise glance over her shoulder. Matilda watched suspiciously from where she stood dusting the curio cabinet. "Mum?"

"Did you see a man come out of the maze? Who is he?"

"The maze, mum?"

"Yes, didn't you see him? A man followed me out of the maze."

"I did not, mum." The maid sniffed at the thought. "I've been here taking care of my duties."

Elise licked her lip as she continued to study the opening of the maze. Disappointed, she dropped the curtain. "Never mind, he has already left."

Matilda walked to the window and peeked out. "You mean him, mum?" The maid's voice raised in question.

Elise looked again and could just see the back of a man hurrying across the yard. She nodded at the sight of the raincoat.

"That's the new gardener."

Relief flooded her at Matilda's confirmation. Of course he was. Things did have to be attended to, after all, no matter what tragedy had happened. She was about to drop the curtain when she noticed the man turn back to look behind him.

She gasped. It wasn't the same man she'd seen in the maze.

Elise backed away from the French doors.

Matilda frowned as she watched. "You okay, mum?"

Elise could barely nod, trying to appease Matilda. Feeling sick, she headed out of the room.

# Chapter 9

Elise headed up the stairs, rubbing her arms. As she passed the statue, she reached out to touch the blue globe, deep in thought. *Who was that man in the maze?* Then, she remembered he'd said his name was Charles, the gardener's helper. Suddenly she felt foolish. *He was probably out there with the new gardener. I just didn't see him is all.*

*I just need to settle down and not get rattled so easily. Keep my guard up, but at the same time, my stress down.*

Elise eyed the original room she was put in as she walked down the hallway. The yellow tape had fallen on one end and someone had wound it around the door handle.

Suddenly, curiosity got the best of her and she decided to take another peek. Maybe there was something the police could have missed? She shrugged and unwound the tape enough to open the door. *It could happen.*

She closed it quickly behind her and glanced around the room. The bathroom door had been left partially open, giving a sliver of a glimpse of the shower curtain. Elise winced at the memory and walked over to the door to firmly shut it. It made her wonder how the investigation was going, trying to track down the derelict.

She looked around the room. Something had to be here, something had to have prompted her to come check again. What was it? She scanned the floor, the bed with its new bedspread that had been brought out just for her, at the walls and the dresser.

Nothing seemed out of the ordinary.

She looked again, feeling like she was a kid studying those black and white drawings of "Can you find what's different?"

*Hmmm.* Something with the wallpaper down there at the corner of the room? That was it. That was what bugged her. Looking again, she couldn't find anything wrong that she hadn't already noticed last night. With a shrug, she tried to brush the nagging feeling off and study something else. But no matter how hard she tried, she kept coming back to that corner. Something there bothered her, but what?

*Take your time.* Her head tipped as she studied it.

The wallpaper was a simple pattern of roses growing up a trellis. Pinks and reds mixed with different shades of green. She walked over and squatted down. What was that? One section of roses grew in a different direction. She ran her fingers around the flowers. A tingle of excitement zinged in her stomach as her fingertip detected a very faint ridge.

She crouched closer. The ridge was nearly indiscernible, looking like it had been smoothed down with a razor blade. She rubbed it again and attempted to get a fingernail under it. After picking at the edge a few times, it slowly curled up.

She sucked in her breath and carefully pulled it away. The paper peeled back revealing squiggly stripes of glue, now yellow with age. Hidden behind it was a little hollow.

Elise leaned to peek inside the hole, just over an inch in height by four inches wide. Someone had removed a chunk of the lathe and plaster to create it. The entrance was thick with dust and cobwebs, though how cobwebs got behind the paper, Elise had no idea.

She plucked her phone from her pocket and swept the light across the opening. The illumination danced across something, making a shadow. She nearly squealed in excitement when she realized it was a book. Carefully, she pulled it out.

The book was about the size of a tiny ledger or address book. Stamped on the front cover was a tree made of gold foil. She blew off the dust and opened it up.

The pages felt like old autumn leaves. The first page was dated November 23, 1937, and stated simply, *Charles has come home.*

Elise brought the book to the bed. Light from the window cast an eerie orange glow, almost giving her the feeling that somehow she'd fallen back in time. She gingerly sat down and the mattress springs protested under her weight.

She scooted back against the headboard and began to read.

*Charles has come home. My darling brother. I could hardly believe my eyes when I received today's letter from Mama. It's been over two years since I last saw him, looking so thin and frail on his way to war. I suspect a lot has changed but when I'll get to see him, I do not know. My post as governess is through to next year, but Papa has promised me that he will have me home by Christmas.*

*Love, Constance*

*Dear Diary*

*Christmas seems so far away. It's been three months, but it feels like it's been forever. Still, I'll not complain. I look around my room now and wonder. I'm blessed to have my own room. So many servants are not afforded these luxuries. But I suspect being a governess has its benefits. Still, I'm scared and alone. Anna and Myrtle are good girls and hardly any trouble.*

*Except.... Do I dare say it? One of them has a sassy streak. I hardly dare write it in case this book is found and becomes public.*

*Ever your servant,*

*Constance.*

Elise flushed with quiet excitement at the treasure in her hands. Here were the very words her great, great grandma had said, perhaps sitting in this very room. Her eyes narrowed. No, this couldn't have been her room. How did the diary get stashed here?

"Elise? Elise? Where are you? Where is that dag-nabbit girl?" Aunt Myrtle's voice wavered with volume, before settling down into a grumble.

Elise looked around, suddenly feeling guilty. She shoved the diary partially into her front pants pocket and adjusted her shirt to cover the top. Footsteps came closer, along with the sharp thump of a cane. Elise jumped up and smoothed the bed's duvet. She spied the curl of wallpaper on the floor. Too late. Aunt Myrtle was pounding on the door across the hall, her room.

"Elise?"

"I'm right here, Aunt Myrtle," Elise said as she opened the door. The old woman staggered back with her hand over her heart. Her mouth hung open with the slackness of shock. "What are you doing in there?" She pointed with a trembling finger. "Did Anna call you?"

"What? No. I was just checking. I should have asked you before making myself welcome. I'm sorry I scared you."

Aunt Myrtle opened and shut her mouth a few times. She took a deep breath before plucking her white cardigan down where it had become rumpled. "It's fine. Be careful in that room. Don't make Anna upset."

Elise found herself nodding in agreement, not understanding at all. "Yes, yes, of course. Was there something you needed?"

The old woman leaned on her cane.

"I mean, just now, when you were calling for me?" Aunt Myrtle didn't answer so Elise tried again, "Did you have a good time at Cribbage Club?"

"I came home early because I got news." Aunt Myrtle pulled a cell phone out of the pocket of her skirt. "On one of these newfangled things. People can get ahold of you anywhere, these days. Anyway, my son's coming home."

This was news. "Coming home? To stay?"

"I'm not sure. It's his birthday soon. Maybe he's here for a present. I wouldn't put it past him. At any rate, those kids should come home and stay. It's high time for them to settle down now and quit all this lollygagging like a tourist in foreign countries."

"He's touring? I thought he owned the family company."

"Oh, he and his sister think they're in charge. But really, it's still under my control." Aunt Myrtle's eyes stared intently at Elise. "My board of directors keep me updated. They've wanted me to step down for years."

"They?"

"My children. Stephen and Caroline. But they'll get their hands on it soon enough." The old lady turned and began hobbling back down the hall. "When I'm good and dead. Now, follow me."

# Chapter 10

Elise did exactly what the old lady ordered and followed her out to the hallway. Before she shut the door, she wound the caution tape tightly around the doorknob.

"How long is that ugly yellow thing going to be there anyway?" Aunt Myrtle took one look at it and sniffed.

"Until the police are done with their investigation."

"What good is it for, anyway? Looks more like a flag for bull."

"It's to keep people out." Elise felt her cheeks heat with a guilty flush.

Aunt Myrtle snorted. "You look like you just ate the canary. The tape didn't do too good, I reckon?"

Elise cleared her throat and glanced down the hall. "What was it you wanted to show me, again?"

"Hmph. I wanted to show you what Anna's after." She thumped her cane on the floor as she slowly walked to her dead sister's room. "You heard her the other night, right?"

"Well, Anna's gone. How could I have heard her?"

"Anna's always been that way. She does what she wants."

Prickles crawled up Elise's arm as they entered the room. It felt darker than ever before. "Why are you saying that? Have you seen her?"

The old woman licked her dry pale lips. "Well, no. But it has to be her." She thumped her way over to the dollhouse. A smile lit up her face. Turning, she looked proudly at Elise.

"This is lovely," Elise peered inside the house, trying to appear as if it were the first time she'd seen it up close.

"We need more light." Aunt Myrtle batted at the curtain with her cane, and Elise rushed over to open it. Something clattered in the bathroom, making Elise jump. "Hold your horses, Anna. I'm just showing her." Then turning her attention back to Elise, "My Grandfather made it for me."

"For you and not your sister?"

"Yes. It was for my fifth birthday. I loved it. It sat for nearly seventy years in my room." Her forehead crinkled into an impossible map of wrinkles. "Anna always was so jealous of it. She played with it one day, and broke the tiny cradle." Her bony finger reached in and touched the chair. "Mother was mad at me for it. I'd told her it wasn't me, but Mother didn't believe me. Anna, of course, never said otherwise."

Sympathy filled Elise at the pain in Aunt Myrtle's voice. "Oh, I'm sorry. That must have been hard."

"Hard?" The old woman looked confused. "No, it wasn't hard. That was Anna."

"So, you didn't get along with your sister then?"

Aunt Myrtle looked to the floor and a pink hue tinged her cheeks. "Anna was just the prettiest thing. You'd fall in love with her right away if you'd seen her, just like everyone else did. Hair like a buttercup. Eyes like two violets. Just beautiful." Myrtle cleared her throat. "Momma always said Anna must have the pink dress. I was always dressed in blue."

"The blue?"

"Yes," Myrtle looked at her again, "On account of my hair." She touched it, now thin with pink scalp showing through the white curls.

"You have lovely hair, Myrtle," Elise remarked.

Myrtle blinked and then looked sharply at Elise. "Do you have beetles for brains? What are you babbling about?" Her tone flipped from the softness it had previously.

"I was saying your hair.... It's quite beautiful."

Myrtle looked at her as though Elise were crazy. "My hair is about as beautiful as a bud of blown cotton tumbling in a muddy cow pasture. And nobody has ever called it beautiful. Plain, they said. Just plain brown. Besides that, any beauty that my hair had is long gone, now." She scowled at Elise and turned back to the bedroom door, gripping her cane in a gnarled hand and leaving Elise to follow behind bemused.

***

A half-hour later, carrying a small knapsack with a water bottle and a jacket, Elise climbed in her car and drove to Highjack Ridge. Her brain spun with Aunt Myrtle's last conversation. She turned up the music to clear her thoughts. *Not going to let anything distract me from today. It's time to recharge.*

Brad's jeep was already waiting in the park's dirt parking lot when she pulled in. She took the space next to him and climbed out with her knapsack.

He walked over and she felt her heart smile. He looked every bit as wonderful as the last time she'd seen him. Something about him just emanated security and confidence, and not just because she knew he was a police officer. He was a good man. It just radiated from him.

And his hugs were the best.

So far, they hadn't gone any further in their relationship other than friendship, still feeling things out and getting to know each other. But Elise liked the way they were headed.

"Long time, no see," he said, grabbing her in his arms.

"Mmmmmm," she responded, snuggling in. His arms were strong and tight and he smelled like cedar. She looked up at his face. "Have you been chopping wood?"

He grinned. "Look at you, Miss Detective. Solving two mysteries has sure honed your skills. Yep, I had a cord and a half delivered. Trying to get my winter pile in shape."

"You split wood this morning and now you're going to hike a mountain? You are a beast."

His eyebrow flickered. "I've gotta do a lot to make sure I impress you," he joked.

"Hey, you already impressed me when we did that half-marathon last month."

"Yeah? Well, I have a few more tricks up my sleeve."

"Oh, really?"

Leaving her question unanswered, he moved to his jeep and pulled out a back pack. "Come on, let's get going." He slid it on as he nodded toward the trailhead.

Elise shrugged her pack on and followed him. Just a few feet down the trail and Elise felt the shift. Life suddenly felt rugged and wild in direct opposite of the civilization of the parking lot. Enormous evergreens reached for the sky for as far as she could see. She sniffed deeply. The mountain air was so fresh. An old river bed cut across the path. She glanced at the ground to be sure of her footing as she crossed the boulders.

They traveled with minimal small talk for the first two miles, both of them recharging in the quiet of the countryside. The trail leveled out and they crossed a field of yellow flowers.

"I can't believe how beautiful it is here," Elise said, unable to help herself. She did a slow spin, trying to take it all in. When she turned back he had plucked a blossom and held it between his fingers. Smiling, he took her hand and drew her close. His hazel eyes were warm as he looked into hers and he tucked the flower behind her ear. "Spoken by a true beauty." He bent down to kiss her.

Warmth flooded Elise as his lips pressed against hers. She wrapped her arms around his neck and kissed him back.

After a few moments, they parted, both smiling. She rested her head on his shoulder as he hugged her again. "You can't even believe how long I've been wanting to do that," he said.

"Really?" Reluctantly, she stepped away

"Probably since high school." His eyes twinkled as his hand ran down her arm. He grabbed her hand and gave it a squeeze before readjusting his back pack.

"High school, huh?"

"Right from Mr. Thompson's Algebra class." He laughed. "You sat in front of me, always looking so cute. I blame you for getting such low grades that year."

"Whatever!" Elise rolled her eyes and pulled out a water bottle. She took a long drink.

"Still another thousand feet to the top. You ready?" he said. She offered him the bottle and he took a swig too before passing it back.

She nodded and returned the bottle, then pulled out two cherry suckers. He looked at it with an eyebrow raised as she handed one over. "Try it," she smiled. "They're organic and a little pick-me-up. I need a little bit of sugar halfway through a hike."

"I just gave you a little sugar," he joked and stuck the sucker in his mouth. Winking at her, he started up the trail.

She snorted and followed after him.

The climb was steep and finally dwindled into steps carved into the path. Every step was an exclamation point of pain in her back, shoulders, and legs.

"Almost there," Brad encouraged. At this point, Elise was too tired to even look around, instead stared at the back of Brad's legs and sneakers. *One more step. I can do this. Just one more step. I lied. One more step.*

Finally, they made it, both of them grinning as the whole valley opened up below them.

"Can you see that over there? That's the Penny Wiggle grocery store." Brad pointed. "Look, that's the police department."

"There's my neighborhood," Elise added, dropping her pack.

"Yep. And over there is Montgomery Manor."

Elise studied it, seeing the neighboring house. She never realized how close Uncle Shorty lived to the mansion. "What's that behind it? The golf course?"

Brad snorted. "Well, people are dying to get in there. That's the back of the cemetery."

She looked at it and shivered, despite the sun beating on her sweaty skin and Brad's corny joke.

"You nervous or something?" Brad asked. "You can't be cold."

"No. It's just that house is a little creepy. I mean, hello? First a dead body and now there's a cemetery right behind it."

"Yeah, well that brings up something I've been wanting to talk to you about."

"What?"

"You ever think about taking a self-defense class? There's one called Safety First starting next week at the Gilmore Village. I was thinking...." he trailed off, looking questioningly at her.

Elise shook her head. "Nah, it's not something I'm interested in. At. All," she punctuated vehemently.

Brad gave her a raised eyebrow look. "Why on earth not? I think everyone should know some basic self-defense. It would be great for you. Actually, it'd make me feel better too."

"I don't know, really. It makes me feel silly somehow."

"Why?" He sat on a boulder and pulled out his cell to snap some photos of the valley.

"Well," Elise wrinkled her nose. "It's just the way I imagine it. The yelling. The getting aggressive with someone."

"Sometimes you need to. You have a voice, You don't have to be afraid to use it."

"I know, I know."

"Just tell me that you'll think about it." He aimed the phone at her and snapped a shot with a smile. "Man, I'm going to miss you."

"I know, me too. When do you leave?"

"Monday. Two more days."

"You're only going to be gone for one more week, right? And then you're done with training for good?" Her voice ended wistfully.

"Just one week. How much trouble can you get into?" He glared at her and held up a finger. "Don't answer that."

# Chapter 11

Elise drove to the manor after the hike, still filled with that butterfly-giddy feeling. *For crying out loud, I'm like a teenager getting her first kiss.* She smiled. In a way, that's exactly how it felt. Indescribably wonderful.

Tree branches bounced with the wind. Rain started, landing in fat splats on the windshield. She flipped the wipers on. *Oh, boy. Time for some new ones.* The old wipers left streaky arcs across the glass.

Should she take Brad up on the self-defense class? It bothered her that her first reaction was to be repelled at the idea. But, at the same time, thinking about yelling and hitting anyone, even a trained teacher, intimidated her.

She pulled down the driveway to the manor. Most of the lights on the upper floors were off, despite it only being nine. Everyone, including the staff, seemed to go to bed early here. They'd probably been doing it since before Aunt Myrtle was born. A structure the whole family never thought to vary.

Elise shifted the car into park and studied the mansion through the windshield. Such a strange place. Both lonely and majestic at the same time. So full of history. What would happen to the Manor when Aunt

Myrtle died? Would her kids keep it? They didn't appear that interested, considering how little they visited.

Those kids seemed like a whole other story. Why would children abandon their aging mother? Was it just the selfishness of young adulthood, trying to find their way in the world? That stage in life where they thought they knew it all?

Or was there something else?

Shaking her head, Elise climbed out of the car. Rain hit her hard, and she ran up to the front steps with her hands covering her hair. Her clothing was quite wet by the time she got to the door.

She tried the key in the lock and let herself inside. The hall was quiet and dark, dimly illuminated by several wall sconces.

Quickly, she hurried up the stairs, her wet clothing feeling like it was shrinking against her skin. As she rounded the landing, her hand unconsciously dropped to touch the blue globe on the statue. She stopped as if struck.

It was gone.

*What in the world?* She looked again. The globe was nowhere in sight. Squatting down, she grabbed out her cell phone and used the flashlight to look behind the statue. Nothing. She ran the light along the wall in both directions to see if it had somehow fallen and rolled.

*What the heck could have happened to it? Had somebody knocked it off and was just waiting to replace it later? Or was this what Charlotte was referring to when she said things disappeared?*

Feeling slightly discombobulated, she continued on up the rest of the stairs. The blank spot in the middle of the portraits on the hallway wall seemed to yell at her as she passed. She shook her head and entered her bedroom, locking the door behind her.

Once in the bathroom, she peeled off the wet jeans and hung them over the shower curtain rod. After pulling her shirt over her head, she caught a glimpse of herself in the bathroom mirror and laughed. Her hair looked like it had been licked by a cow with the way it stuck straight up in the back. She grabbed a hair brush off the counter and smoothed it down.

A clunk stopped her actions. Elise froze, listening. Was that back out in the hall? She walked into her bedroom and listened again. Nothing. *Maybe my running to my room sent a picture off the wall?* She reached for her bathrobe and slipped it on, then opened her door and shone the cell's flashlight at the portraits. Nope. With the exception of the missing one, all of them were in place.

She flashed the light in the other direction. What was that? For a second it looked like a light flickered from under the bedroom door that had once belonged to Anna. Her muscles tensed with nerves before she shook them off and marched over to the room. *I'm going to figure out what's going on here once and for all.* She grabbed the doorknob and twisted.

It was locked.

Elise shook the knob to see if it was jammed, then shook it again in indignation that someone would lock it. There was no response. She knocked on the door and held her ear against it to listen. Nothing. Scratching the back of her neck, she backed away, staring at the offending handle. Had she accidentally locked it on her way out that last time? No, she was certain she'd just closed the door behind her.

She knocked again, harder this time. "Is anyone in there?"

The butler came around the corner. "Ma'am?" he asked, his voice tinged with sleepiness.

"I think someone might be in there," Elise explained, pointing to the room.

"Who'd be in there at this time of night?" Hamilton's face went stiff as he fought off a yawn.

"I'm not sure who, but I saw a light under the door. And look, now it's locked." To demonstrate, she twisted the handle.

It fell away from under her hand as the door swung open. Her mouth dropped as the Butler looked at her with one eyebrow raised. Shaking her head in confusion, Elise ignored him and entered the room.

Crossing over the floor, she turned on the lamp. She glanced around and tried the windows. Everything appeared the same.

"If there's nothing else, ma'am?" The butler asked as he peered throughout the room inside, seeming to assure himself that Elise was just a crazy person and that there was obviously no one was in the room.

"No," Elise hesitated before sending him a big smile. "I'm so sorry that I woke you. My eyes must have been playing tricks on me."

Hamilton nodded. "It is late, ma'am. Perhaps it was a nightmare?" She raised her eyebrows at his ridiculous statement. "If there's nothing else?"

Elise shook her head in the negative.

With a brief tip his head in acknowledgment, Hamilton turned down the hall.

Elise raked her fingers through her hair and held it as a feeling of frustration bubbled through her. Despite what she'd just said, she'd never had her eyes play tricks on her like that. She could have sworn she saw flickering light, like a candle, tickling the bottom edge of the bedroom door. She stared at her cell phone. *Did you somehow reflect on something down there?*

She glanced at the time. Well, it wasn't that late, but it was late enough that she should probably take her shower and get into bed.

The dollhouse stood just as majestic as ever framed by the light of the lamp. She considered it for a moment, thinking of the picture on the wall. Just for the sake of curiosity, she walked over. Leaning down, she searched for the statue on the stairwell and smiled when she found it. She still couldn't believe the perfect detail that was captured here in miniature. Yep, there it was on the stair's landing.

A chill ran down her back.

The fairy stared blankly, its hand empty of the blue sphere.

# Chapter 12

Elise hurried from the room texting Brad, her skin crawling with the heebie-jeebies. With a few short sentences, she quickly filled him in. His response was just as fast, insisting that he come over right then and check things out. Through massive persuasion, she managed to push his visit off to the next day. She already knew how Aunt Myrtle felt about the police. Surely the old woman wouldn't be pleased to have one in her house at this time of night, even if it was Elise and Lavina's friend.

Needing some time to settle down, she took a shower, letting the warm water push away the chills and confusion. Afterward, she brushed her hair and braided it, hoping against hope to avoid another restless night of sleep.

***

Just after lunchtime the next day, Brad pulled up the long drive in his official police car. Elise cringed, hoping Aunt Myrtle wouldn't be embarrassed. As Elise hurried down the stairs, she could already hear the buzz his appearance created. The butler let Brad in, cutting off the whispers from the two maids watching from the foyer.

Brad gave Hamilton a quick nod as he came in, and his eyes caught Elise's.

"You're in your gear," she noted. Their hug felt awkward with the various police equipment poking into her, and Brad's chest stiff with armor.

"Just about to start my shift and wanted to stop by." He looked up the stairwell. "Come on, show me."

She grabbed his hand and led him up.

"Where's Myrtle?" he asked, his heavy boots clumping on the polished stairs.

"Watch out for the—"

Too late. He hit the creaky step and jerked at the sharp sound. "Geez!"

"I tried to warn you." Elise paused next to the statue. "So, here is one of the missing items."

"Did you ask anyone where it could be?" he questioned, pulling on a pair of leather gloves. Squatting next to it, he examined the base of statue.

"No, not yet. I just noticed it last night."

He stood again and ran a finger around the empty hands of the fairy. Nodding, he said, "Okay. What's the next thing?"

Together, they examined the line of portraits, then on to the dollhouse. He ducked under the yellow tape and glanced around the room and then the bathroom where the murdered gardener had been found. After he was satisfied, he crossed the hall to her room. He tested the lock on her bedroom door and made sure the windows were secure.

"You make sure you lock this at night." He scooped her into his arms and gave her a hard stare. "I'm already worried about you."

"I do, and don't worry. I've got this."

He arched an eyebrow and gently tucked a stray hair behind her ear. "I think I've heard that one before."

"I swear, I'll be fine. Now come on." She walked him back out to his car.

"So," Elise hesitated as Brad jiggled his keys. Neither one made a move to leave. "Do you think Aunt Myrtle's crazy?"

Brad's eyebrow jerked at the word. He ran his hand over his chin and glanced up at the house. Finally, he shook his head. "No. I'm not sure what's going on here, but I think that woman is as sharp as a tack."

"Even though she's insisting her sister's haunting her?"

He sighed. "I don't know. I can't say I haven't heard strange stories like that before. She may be a little off there, but something is going on. Something I don't like you being in the middle of." He hooked his fingers around hers and smiled. "Have you given any more thought to that defense class?"

Elise shook her head. Just the mention of it had her on edge. "It's just not me."

"What part's not you? The defending part?"

"I think I could do pretty good on my own. I don't feel like getting up in front of everyone to yell and attack someone."

"Yeah, but they're all there to do the same thing. And it's the instructor's job to come under fire like that."

"He'll be yelling back." She rubbed her neck as sweat broke out. "I don't know. I just can't do it."

Brad nodded. "Well, I know you can do it. You're a lot stronger than you think. Look at you, swimming in the Atlantic ocean."

Elise snorted. Over near the driveway's edge, a Canadian goose landed with its partner. They waddled and honked, their beaks turning over dead leaves for insects. Ignoring the distraction, she turned back to Brad.

"I was pretty drugged up, remember?" she responded. "And my training kicked in."

Brad let go of her hand and reached around her shoulders. "That's right. You proved my point." Elise groaned as he went on. "Defense training is the same way. They're just tools that kick in when you need them."

"Fine. I'll think about it." She sighed, with a reluctant half-smile.

"That's what I wanted to hear." He pulled her in closer and tipped his head down, giving her a kiss. Her fingers wound their way into his hair and she melted into him.

He pulled away with a satisfied smile. "Keep thinking about it. I'll see you in a week."

"Think about what?" she joked back as he climbed into his car. She waved as he backed out of the driveway.

Elise jogged up the porch steps grinning to herself.

***

Back in her room, Elise grabbed the diary and stuck it in her pocket with the full intent of finding some cozy spot outside to read it. Instead, curiosity grabbed her and she ended up walking towards the parlor.

There was a room on the other side she wanted to explore. As she entered, she was filled with delight. It was the library.

Inside the door sat a bust of Cleopatra. Her hair swooped in ivory curls over her left shoulder as she stared straight ahead. Elise couldn't resist touching it, smiling a little at the cool stone.

Built into the tower, the library walls curved around her, stacked with shelves of books. Overhead was a chandelier that lent a sparkling warm glow throughout the cozy space. The entire room was small; it only took her ten steps to cross over to the bookshelves on the other side.

Leather bound books stood at attention, in colors of red, brown, and black. She perused the titles and let out a soft chuckle. Titles reminiscent of her awkward pre-teen years were like old friends. Anne of Green Gables. Little Women.

She stooped to examine the lower shelf. Here were children's books, standing in line like a colorful rainbow. Probably kept at this height by Aunt Myrtle's father hoping to entice his children. She looked higher and there were the more serious titles; a book of Atlases, Ulysses, books on war, and the Bible.

A nook filled with cushions enticed her and she meandered over. Settling down, she glanced out the latticed window at the rolling green lawn and the driveway lined with maples. *So peaceful. I bet Myrtle was the reader. I wonder how many times she sat here herself?*

Elise pulled the diary out from her pocket with the feeling like the sunlight sifting through the window was turning back time. It could have been seventy years ago. Everything still looked the same.

A thread dangled from where she'd left it on the last page she'd read.

*Dear Diary*

*Today was a lovely day. The Christmas festivities were in full swing last night with the tree lighting and Christmas caroling. I accompanied the family to keep an eye on Myrtle. The sweet little thing was all bundled up, and still her nose and cheeks were red.*

*And I was even surprised by Mr. Montgomery with a pair of slippers! My first pair. I can hardly believe how soft and warm they are.*

*I did get to go home for a quick visit, but it was much too brief. Still, I was able to hug Charles. He was thin but looked so good. Mama and Papa looked good too, as well as Elizabeth and her husband and children. I confess, I can't wait to get married one day and have a brood of my own.*

*Still, I don't mind if that day stays a bit in the future. I absolutely adore Myrtle. She is a bit precocious but absolutely precious. She made me an embroidered handkerchief, and I will never treasure a gift more. I know well how much she detests sitting still and the poor cotton square is dotted with her blood.*

*I am a blessed woman.*

*Yours-*

*Constance*

A throat clearing jarred Elise. She jerked up from the book, feeling slightly bug-eyed.

"I wondered when I'd find you in here." Aunt Myrtle stood in the doorway staring at her curiously. She toddled forward, her cane tapping on the old, polished floor, her knitting in a satchel over her arm. "This was one of my favorite places growing up."

Elise shifted her feet to the floor and sat up, trying to surreptitiously hide the diary. "I can see why. It's so beautiful and peaceful."

Tap. Tap. Tap. Aunt Myrtle crossed over to the book shelf. As she looked up at the books her face softened with a wistful yearning. Elise could almost catch a glimmer of the little girl she'd once been.

"I'd come in here with Papa. He's the one that put all of these books on this shelf for me. Every year for Christmas, he'd add three more." She read off a few of the titles. "Robinson Crusoe. Oliver Twist, Moby Dick. Doctor Dolittle."

"Did you read all those?" Elise asked, replacing the diary in her pocket.

"I did, many times over. Sitting right where you are now." Aunt Myrtle ran a shaky finger down the edge of the shelf. "These are dusty."

"I noticed the stairs are as well. I was thinking of going over them for you."

"They are?" The old woman pressed her mouth together, and lines like cat's whiskers formed at her lips.

"My vision isn't what it used to be. Those two flibbertigibbets. They come and go around here."

"Your housekeepers? Are they new?"

"New enough. They stay long enough for me to properly train them, then off they fly to get married, or some convoluted thing like that." Aunt Myrtle sighed. "I supposed I'll have Hamilton speak to them. Though why he hasn't yet, I'll never know. He's been off his game too, lately."

"Maybe…" Elise swallowed and then finished with a rush, "the death of the gardener has them shaken?"

"Could be true. You can't get used to seeing death no matter how many times it happens." Aunt Myrtle thumped over and sat in the wing-back chair, dropping the satchel on the floor next to her. "Speaking of such, I saw you had a copper here again today."

"Oh, that was my friend. He was just saying goodbye before he took off for training."

"Your friend, huh?" Aunt Myrtle sniffed. "Or, is he your romantic interest?"

"Oh," Elise couldn't help the smile. "You could say that, but it's new."

"My parents had plans for Shorty to be my intended paramour. But I had other ideas."

"Other ideas, like Mr. Kennington?" Elise smiled.

Aunt Myrtle chuckled. "New York City in the '50s was a thing to behold. That man knew how to cut a rug. Won me over before the jitterbug ended." Her smile fell away. "This place hasn't been the same without him."

Elise looked down at the floor. "I'm sorry about that."

"Oh? What are you sorry for? It's the way of life. It's just that since he's been gone, Anna's been back with a vengeance."

Elise's chest tightened at the name of Aunt Myrtle's sister. She spun her earring a few times. "That brings up another reason why my friend came this morning. There's been something else that's disappeared. He wanted to see if he could find a clue as to where it went."

Aunt Myrtle shifted in her chair until she could see Elise. She held her cane in both hands. "What's missing?"

"Um," Elise swallowed, unsure of what the older woman would think. "You know the fairy statue?"

Aunt Myrtle closed her eyes. "I'm listening."

"The blue globe that one of the fairies was holding has disappeared."

Aunt Myrtle sighed and turned away, but not before Elise noticed the older woman's bottom lip tremble. "That was my favorite statue. Papa bought it for me as a wedding gift, along with the one for my dollhouse. The blue sphere was my favorite color, and stood for hope and valor."

The older woman sniffed and reached into her pocket to retrieve her lace hanky. Patting under her eyes, she continued, "Does that mean my hope is gone?"

"No, no. Of course not." Elise stood from the window seat and walked over to wrap her arm around Aunt Myrtle's shoulders. "Do you have any idea who would have done such a thing?"

The old lady pressed the cotton square to her mouth and closed her eyes tightly. She seemed to be holding her breath to try and keep her emotions contained. After a moment, she nodded, just a stiff bob of the head.

"Who?" Elise pressed.

"Anna. She was always so jealous of me."

This was the second time Myrtle had mentioned her sister's jealousy. Elise couldn't understand it. Jealous of what? Of a little girl with scrapes on her knees constantly getting into trouble with their mother?

"Do you know why?" Elise asked again.

Aunt Myrtle cleared her throat and with a slight motion of her shoulders, shrugged Elise's arm off. She stuck her chin in the air. "Anna was jealous of Papa's and my relationship. She never could see how Papa adored her, too." Aunt Myrtle glanced down at her handkerchief and proceeded to refold it. "Of course, with her being his first child, and always under Mother's thumb to be a proper lady, I don't deny he was awkward with her. He hardly knew what to do with a young woman about to be presented to the world. He worried for her match." Aunt Myrtle looked at Elise. "But me, I was easy for him. I was rough and tumble and covered in dirt."

"It sounds like maybe he treated you like a son?" Elise murmured.

"Perhaps that's how he saw me." Aunt Myrtle tucked the folded linen square back in her pocket. "But all that changed after Anna died. Papa left for his business. That's why that statue was so important to me. Because he brought it to me when he came back home for good. And he came back in every way."

"In every way?" Elise felt confused at the wording.

Aunt Myrtle nodded. "Yes. When he left he was a shadow of his former self, but when he came back, he was his normal loving and enthusiastic self. He used to play with Stephen—this was before Caroline was born—and they played all sorts of spy games together, with pretend pirate treasure. Papa used his coins, you know, that he had collected throughout the years. The two of them would hide the coins and pretend people were out to steal them." She smiled, her eyes twinkling. "He sure loved that boy. Poor Caroline, she missed so much. She was only a baby when he died."

Elise settled back in the window seat. Rain lashed against the window pane. "Your father sounds like a wonderful man."

"He was." Aunt Myrtle agreed. "And then he was gone. Then Mother was gone, and it was just me and Mr. Kennington. And then he was gone too."

Elise felt her heart squeeze at so much loss being rattled off like a grocery list. "I'm so sorry."

Aunt Myrtle sighed and reached for her glasses. She perched them on her nose and scooped up her knitting onto her lap from the satchel at the foot of the chair. "What can you do? It's the way of life. You live. You die. You're supposed to move on." Her lips silently moved as she counted her stitches on the needle. "Which is why it's so torturous that Anna has not."

# Chapter 13

The two sat together in the quiet of the library for about twenty minutes, Aunt Myrtle knitting and Elise watching the rain out the window. The cuckoo clock chimed two o'clock, making both women look up.

"Well, I've had just about enough of this," said Aunt Myrtle, winding up her yarn and tucking it back into the basket. "I'm feeling a bit peckish. Care for a bite to eat?"

Elise stood up and stretched, surprised at how cramped her legs suddenly felt. "That sounds great." She yawned with her arms still in the air.

Aunt Myrtle pursed her lips. "You keep your mouth wide open like that, you're liable to catch a bird. In my day, ladies did not stretch like lumberjacks."

Elise dropped her arms immediately from the sting of the scolding. She followed the elderly woman out of the room and down the hall.

When they passed the dining room, Elise arched an eyebrow in surprise. Aunt Myrtle led her down the hall and through the kitchen, past the counters stacked with various kitchen gadgets, past the hanging shining copper pans, until she finally stopped at a bay window off to the side. A little round table with two chairs sat there.

"This is where I like my special tea," Aunt Myrtle said primly as she rested a trembling hand on a ladder-back chair. She dragged the chair out, frowning as the wooden legs jittered on the floor from her shaking.

"Here, let me help you," Elise pulled it out carefully so as not to knock the old lady off balance.

Aunt Myrtle's lips tightened and she didn't acknowledge the help. She sat as soon as the chair was out and propped her cane on the side of the table. "Now, let's have some tea and talk a spell."

Cookie came over with a tray holding a china tea pot dotted with tiny pink flowers, two cups and saucers, and a cream and sugar set. The cook's face was flushed and tiny gray curls escaped around the edges of her mop cap. "Good afternoon, mum. Fancy seeing you here today. Summer's come twice since you were here last."

"Well, it's still my favorite place. And don't you forget it," Aunt Myrtle snapped. "Now, where are my fresh flowers?"

Cookie looked even more flustered and hurried across the kitchen to hold a fiercely whispered conversation with Charlotte. The young maid looked chastised as she bobbed her head and fled the room.

"They're right on their way, mum," Cookie assured, walking over to the bread box. She returned with a plate filled with dainties: little cookies with maraschino cherries pressed in their centers and crescent shaped biscuits dipped in powdered sugar and sprinkled with shaved almonds. The cook set the plate down before turning it in a more pleasing direction towards Aunt Myrtle and stood back with her hands clasped behind her. "Will there be anything else, mum? Shall I make some cucumber sandwiches?"

Aunt Myrtle picked a flake of almond off the plate and brought it to her mouth. "No. This will be enough. Thank you, Cookie."

The cook bobbed her head, seeming out of breath, and went back to the other end of the kitchen. She pulled a silver bowl from where it had been tucked in the corner and removed the cheese cloth covering it. After assessing the dough's condition, she proceeded to flour the counter and upturn the contents onto its surface.

Aunt Myrtle filled the china cups with tea. Her hand barely shook as she held the lid tight on the teapot. "This was always my favorite place," she said, setting the pot down. She moved her cup closer and reached for an almond biscuit. "Right here, right at the heart of the house. I used to come here when Anna was with Mother. And, I came here even more after Anna died. It was here that I found life." She dipped the biscuit into the tea and took a tiny bite.

"It's a lovely place." Elise admired the nook that looked out at a small herb garden. Rain pattered against the basil leaves. "Very welcoming."

"Yes, welcoming. That was what I needed when I was young. To be seen and welcomed." The older woman set the biscuit on the edge of the saucer. "And then, when I married Frank," Elise's ears perked up. She was so curious about Aunt Myrtle's husband. "I'd come here when he was away on business and the bed had turned into a lonely island that grew colder as the night wore on." She sighed. "Then the children came. My little loves." Her eyes misted at the memories.

"Aww, how precious." Elise fished a cookie off the plate and took a bite. The sweet center filled her mouth, reminding her of so many Shirley Temples she'd had as a kid. *How funny that nostalgia is contagious.*

"I think that was another thing that made Anna jealous."

The cookie seemed to turn to ash in Elise's mouth. She took a sip of tea to wash it down."Jealous? Why?"

"Because I had what she'd always wanted. A home, a family. She always wanted what I had."

Elise frowned. *What an odd thing to say. I just don't get what normal fifteen-year-old would ever be jealous of an eight-year-old?* "If you don't mind me asking, what makes you say that?"

"She didn't like that Papa had hired Constance, your great, great grandma, to take care of me."

"My Grandma didn't take care of Anna, too?"

"No, Constance was mine. All mine. She made up the most fun games. We would race out behind there," she pointed towards the garage. "Where no one could see." Aunt Myrtle looked at her, head tipped. "You know, I still can't get over how much you look like her. Right here, around your mouth. And in your eyes." Aunt Myrtle smiled. "She was the kindest person I'd ever met. It was so hard for me when she was sent away."

"Why was she sent away?"

"When Anna died, nothing was the same again. Mother wanted the house shut down, and she sent everyone away. All except Cookie...." here Cookie looked up from where she was punching dough. "Not you, Cookie," Aunt Myrtle amended. "A different one." She squinted her eyes as she regarded the cook. "A thinner one."

"Oh, my goodness," Elise murmured, cringing. She took another sip to cover her embarrassment.

"What? I didn't mean anything by it. I was just explaining. And that's why the kitchen held life."

"Okay, go on."

"Mother didn't like Constance because she defended me about the missing dollhouse chair. I hadn't lost it, but

Mother didn't believe me. Later, Constance pulled it from her pocket and informed Mother that it had been found. Anna tried to tell Mother that Constance had stolen it, but I knew better."

"Why would Anna steal the chair?"

"Because it was mine. Like I said, she always wanted what was mine."

"You said she came back after you had kids. How do you know?"

"Things started to disappear. Small things. First a baby jacket, then a favorite rattle. Then I saw things in the dollhouse disappear. Just like they had when I was a little girl."

Elise sat straighter. "Like what?"

"Little things. Things that Anna knew I'd admired. A plate of muffins. A few pieces of tiny silverware from the dining room table."

Aunt Myrtle paused and stared straight into Elise's eyes. "Then it became more serious. She left me a message."

The hair on the back of Elise's neck rose. "What did it say?"

"It's not what it said, it's what she meant. Anna knew I'd understand."

"What was the message?" Elise watched the elderly woman's every move.

"It was a pair of bloody footprints that led through my room to the door. I recognized the heel print as shoes she wore as a teenager."

"What do you think she meant?" Freaked out, Elise could barely whisper the words.

"Get out while you can. This house is mine." Aunt Myrtle calmly took another sip of tea.

# Chapter 14

The next morning, Aunt Myrtle was all business. She wanted Elise ready and waiting for her by the car, at exactly eight-thirty sharp.

Elise sent a message with Matilda she'd be skipping breakfast—cringing at the thought of enticing Aunt Myrtle's wrath—and rushed through her morning routine. On the way out the door, she snagged a croissant from the kitchen and hurriedly took bites. She made it to the car with ten minutes to spare.

Aunt Myrtle hadn't arrived yet, but apparently Ernest, the chauffeur, had received the same memo. He stood by the car dressed in his suit, shiny at the knees, and a hat firmly clamped over his head.

"Lovely day, today, ma'am." Ernest greeted her as she approached.

"Hello, Ernest. Ready for a fun day?"

"Driving is always fun with Ms. Kennington."

Elise laughed. "You've worked for her a long time. Seen her children grow up, I suppose?"

"Yes, ma'am. Close to fifty years, I imagine." He smiled slightly as he said that, looking both proud and sentimental at the same time.

"Wow! That's a long time."

"Yes. And my father before me."

"But not your kids?"

"I had a daughter, ma'am. And she worked as a housekeeper before she decided to get married. My grandson was my last hope, but he has chosen another career." He shifted and pressed his chest out.

"Aww, the last of the line." Elise patted his arm.

"It appears that way, ma'am."

"What are you two talking about?" Aunt Myrtle hollered at them, looking especially crotchety this morning as she hobbled towards them. Her legs were tan with thick pantyhose and sensible brown shoes.

"Just telling Ms. Elise that my grandson doesn't work at the Montgomery Manor, ma'am."

"He works at that muscle place, right? All this generation ever thinks about are their phones and muscles. They've lost hold of all of our values we held so dear."

"Yes, ma'am." Ernest held the door open for her and offered his arm so that Aunt Myrtle could grab hold of it and get in the car. Aunt Myrtle waved him off. She fretted with her cane for a moment before finally settling on the seat with a thump surprisingly loud for a diminutive woman. With a grimace, she drew her legs inside and Ernest slowly shut the door.

With his hand hovering a mere millimeter away from Elise's arm, he guided her to the other side and opened the passenger door. The door was shut with the same dignity as the previous one before he climbed in the driver's seat.

"Where to, ma'am?" he asked, addressing Aunt Myrtle through the rear view mirror.

"Bart's Butcher. I'd like to get my son a nice steak." Myrtle situated herself to be more comfortable and crossed her legs at the ankle. She turned to Elise. "Stephen always liked to have steak for his birthday, and I don't trust Cookie with decisions when I need high-quality meat. The last time I sent her, she brought home a piece that was as tough as old shoe leather. You have to know the marbling. That's the key."

"Stephen is due home, ma'am?" Ernest glanced at them in the mirror.

"Yes he is, Ernest, and I hear your grandson is back too."

The old man pulled his gaze from the mirror and stared out the windshield as the car rolled out the driveway. The sun sifted through the trees and dappled the concrete. "Yes, ma'am. I expect they'll meet up."

"Just like old times, eh, Ernest?" Aunt Myrtle's face softened. "Remember how they used to play together? Where did the time fly?"

"I don't know, ma'am. But wherever it went, it took my hair with it."

Aunt Myrtle snorted, and Ernest's face showed a hint of a smile.

"You always were so vain about your hair. You probably greased and pompadoured it away, when you weren't doing your duties."

"That's very true, ma'am." He took the corner slowly, the Lincoln swaying like a bloated whale.

"I remember riding down here on my bike," Aunt Myrtle said as she watched out the window. Her voice dropped softly and Elise leaned closer to hear. "Mother never did like me riding that bike because it wasn't proper. But Papa had said I could, so she didn't fuss too much when he was home." Aunt Myrtle smiled at the memory. "I remember flying down the driveway like I was racing the wind. And at this corner here I'd always ring my bell. I tried to make it every afternoon at three o' clock." Aunt Myrtle's gaze cut away to Elise. "That was when the postman came. Three o'clock sharp. Those were the days when you could depend on a person. Remember that, Ernest."

"Like a heartbeat, that mailman was."

"That's right, and the milkman, too. Every morning at six, we'd hear the bottles rattle on the front stoop. You've never had anything like that cream that rose to the top. But, oh! Would Cookie get mad if it was swiped."

Aunt Myrtle glanced at her again. "That was Cookie One. I guess we are on four now."

"That sounds correct, ma'am" Ernest agreed.

Main Street was crowded with traffic. Ernest pulled up next to the butcher shop and jockeyed the big car into the empty space.

Elise grabbed her sweater, waiting for the car to park. "Whatever happened to your bike?"

Aunt Myrtle's lips pressed together and she shook her head hard. "I'll tell you on the way home. I don't want to speak ill of the dead. Now, come along. Let me teach you how to pick a steak."

Ernest stiffly made his way around the car to open Aunt Myrtle's door. He extended a hand to help her out and then waited as Elise scooted across the seat. Elise slipped on her sweater as she hurried after the old woman who was already half-way up the sidewalk to the butcher's door. Elise got ahead of the old woman just in time to open the door for her.

The bell jingled cheerfully overhead. "Do you want to stop at Lavina's deli on the way back?"

"Well, I don't know dear. We'll see. I do need to stop for my son's favorite cigar. I like to keep them stocked in the humidor for when he comes home. It was my Papa's humidor."

"Ms. Kennington. Nice to see you today." The butcher called from behind a glass case. He looked to be over six feet tall and held a large carving knife. His white apron was stained with streaks of blood, and on the butcher block before him lay a hunk of red meat. "What can I get for you?"

The old woman slowly made her way to the case, her cane beating a tattoo on the worn flooring. "I'm here for a nice rib eye. You have anything fresh today?"

"Do I have anything fresh?" The butcher laughed. "That's like asking does a fish drink water. Of course I've got something fresh." He plunked the knife down and reached into the case, patting a hunk of meat for her attention. "Just look at this baby. Check out the fat grain. It's a beauty."

Aunt Myrtle looked at it sharply before nodding. "That's fine, then, wrap it up. Along with a pound of sausage."

"Coming right up." The butcher brought out a sheet of white paper and began packing up her order.

"As I was saying in the car, Mother didn't like me to ride my bike." Aunt Myrtle continued. "She didn't hold to anything tomboyish. Not like nowadays, where you can be what you want. There were rules then. Structure."

She leaned on her cane. "Anna was always so good about the structure."

"Here you are," the butcher handed over the packages. "On your account?"

"Yes, that's right. What do you think, I'm going to start carrying one of those newfangled credit cards?" The old woman snapped.

The butcher laughed good-naturedly. "I wasn't sure if things had changed." The giant man began to blush. Elise watched, fascinated. "It's just that your bill hasn't been paid the last few months. I'd wondered if something had changed."

"Not paid?" Myrtle frowned. "I'll have my son look into it once he's here." She tucked the packaged under her arm.

"No worries. I'm sure it's just a bank oversight. Have a good day, and say hello to your son for me." the butcher waved.

Myrtle turned to leave, her steps shaky and the bottom of her cane clattering against the floor. She appeared too distracted to respond back. Elise returned the wave and ran to open the door.

"Just you hurry and follow me now." Aunt Myrtle said in a crotchety tone as they got to the street, even though Elise was right behind her. "Ernest? Ernest? Where are you?"

The old man appeared from the front of the car and tipped his hat at the two women. "Right here, ma'am," he said, taking the package and opening the back door. "Did you find what you needed?"

Aunt Myrtle ignored him as she waited by the passenger door. The chauffeur quickly opened it and stood at attention as Aunt Myrtle arranged herself to climb in. Elise followed after.

The ride home was quiet with only Aunt Myrtle instructing Ernest to take them home.. No mention was made of stopping for a cigar or Lavina's deli. Aunt Myrtle watched out the window with a distracted look on her face.

***

Ernest pulled the black Lincoln up the driveway of Montgomery Manor. Elise stared out at the Spanish moss covered trees that lined the driveway. She couldn't get over how it continued to feel like this street of old houses was caught in a loop of time from the past. She half-expected to see little Myrtle flying up the driveway past them, knees pumping, on her bicycle.

She glanced at Aunt Myrtle, who wasn't caught in the same nostalgic thought any longer. The old woman's face was stiff with anger.

"What's the matter, Aunt Myrtle? You seem upset?"

"I just can't understand the missed payment at Bart's Butchers. We Montgomerys have never been late on a payment. Never." She shook her head, her white curls bobbing. "Papa must be rolling in his grave." She glared up at Ernest. "You keep your mouth shut now, Ernest. Don't you pretend to not be eavesdropping."

"Yes, ma'am," the driver said decorously and parked the car. He came to help them out.

Aunt Myrtle went up the stairs, her cane thumping loudly on each tread. "What is this world coming to?" she muttered. "Matilda!" she called before she was all the way in the house. "Ring up Stephen."

Matilda sprang away from the doorway. "Yes, mum. Right away, mum." The maid scampered toward the study. Aunt Myrtle followed, still darkly muttering.

Elise watched for a second before heading up the stairs to her room.

The blank spot on the wall gave her a mild twinge as she walked past. She glanced at her watch. About thirty minutes before lunchtime. *I'll read a bit more of the diary. I'd also like to figure out where Constance's room was. I wonder if it's the small room I saw in the attic of the dollhouse?*

Her room was so welcoming, being situated on the sunny side of the house. Elise walked to the dresser and jiggled open the old top drawer before reaching around in search for the book. She snagged the diary and flipped it open to where she'd left off as she walked to the bed.

Elise was just about to climb on when something grabbed her attention. A shiver of revulsion ran through her.

Laying against the quilted pillow sham was a miniature doll. It was her, wearing the identical clothes she'd worn when she first arrived at the house.

# Chapter 15

Elise picked up the doll and studied it. Same blue jeans with a pink shirt buttoned up the front. Black sneakers tied on the feet. The doll had a painted smile and two green eyes. Its black hair was pulled into a shiny pony tail.

A wave of nausea roiled in Elise's stomach. With great distaste, she carried it between her thumb and forefinger back to the bureau and dropped it on top before wiping her hand on her pants. *What in the world?* She reached in her back pocket for her phone and quickly made a phone call.

"Hi, Brad, I'm surprised you answered. I was planning on leaving you a voice mail," she said when he picked up.

"Hey, beautiful. I have a few minutes between exercises," Brad had dragged out the first word, sounding happy. His voice automatically made her smile. "What's shaking out at the Ghost Manor?"

She shivered. "Worst timing ever. Seriously, that's not funny. But I called to tell you I'm signing up for that class you were talking about."

He let out a surprised sound. "Elise, what's going on?"

Elise stared at the doll again. *Should I tell him or not? Maybe after I talk with someone about it. I don't want to stress him out. Maybe this is somebody's weird idea of a gift.* "It just seems like a good idea after all. Thought it might set your mind at ease while you're at training."

"Awesome! Glad to hear it."

"And, get this. Lavina is doing it with me."

"Wow! How'd you get her to sign up?"

"She doesn't know yet. I'm calling her next."

He chuckled. "Good luck with that." They both talked over the top of each other, saying their goodbyes, before Elise hung up.

She stared at the phone for a second, trying to form a plan of convincing her best friend to join her for the class. Nothing was coming to her. Lavina was too unpredictable and never could be strong-armed into anything. It had made for a teacher's nightmare in high school but served Lavina well as she ran her business.

Elise glanced at the doll on the bureau and shivered. Black hair from the doll's ponytail splayed out on the surface.

*I'm calling, and she's coming with me. That's just the way it's going to be.* Determined, she picked up the phone again and rang Lavina.

Her friend's sassy voice came through the receiver after the first ring. "Good heavens girl, it's only..." there was a pause. "My word, are you calling me at eleven in the morning? That's barely civil."

"I have a big favor to ask you. Huge even."

Without missing a beat, Lavina responded. "Sure, darlin'. Anything."

Elise smiled, knowing Lavina's "anything" might not include getting thrown around by someone dressed like a sumo wrestler. "Want to take a self-defense class with me? It's at Gilmore Village."

The pause on the other end of the phone lasted several seconds. Finally a breathy, "Okay, who are you and what have you done with my friend?"

"What are you talking about?"

"Elise, you've cringed at pillow fights. What do you mean you want to take a self-defense class? What's going on out there? Are you in danger? What's my aunt done to you?"

"Nothing really. Brad mentioned it a few days back and the more I thought about it, the more I thought it might be a good idea." Elise eyed the doll on the dresser and quickly looked away.

"Of course I'll do it with you. When is it?"

Elise was flabbergasted. She walked over to the edge of the bed and sat. "Really? I thought it would be so much harder to talk you into it. It's tomorrow night."

"Aww, you should know me by now. I'm always up for giving a man a good beating." Lavina laughed. "And that gives me just enough time to get a new outfit. What is the proper attire for self-defense? I'm going to need to call my Nordstrom's consultant."

Elise could almost imagine Lavina checking her nails as she spoke. "Lavina, never change."

"I never will, darlin'. Just keep getting better and better."

Elise hung up, feeling lighter than she had in a long time. She replaced the phone in her back pocket. The diary caught her attention again, left open and forgotten on the quilt. She picked it up and scooted back against the headboard to read.

*Dear Diary*

*I saw her today. She didn't know that I saw her, but I did. She slipped the baby from the dollhouse. Later, I saw her outside. She was weeping and wrapping the doll in a corner of a silk handkerchief. She kissed its face and buried it under the old cherry tree that Myrtle likes to climb in the summer. It was then that I knew the rumors were true. Ms. Montgomery had lost the baby. I didn't know what to do? Should I intrude on such a private moment?*

*Poor Anna.*

*Yours,*

*Constance*

Frowning, Elise turned to the next entry

*Dear Diary*

*She did it again today, took another person from the doll house. This one was her Father. Anna tiptoed past the school room as if I wouldn't see her. I couldn't help but try to follow and see where she'd take the doll. She somehow slipped away.*

*Later, Myrtle was awful upset at finding the Father missing. She carried on over dinner, while her mother scolded her for unbecoming actions of a young lady. I watched silently, hardly knowing what to do. Anna never mentioned a word, just sat there silently, eating her dinner. I dare say there was a look of triumph in that girl's eyes. Why would she do that? Do I tattle on Anna? Her mother dotes on her, I'd be surely dismissed from my position. I hardly know what to do.*

*Yours,*

*Constance*

The lunch bell rang, pulling Elise from Constance's world. *You and me both, G. G. Grandma. I don't know what to do either.* She found a thread and laid it between the pages, then shut the book. What was going on with Anna back then? Why take the house's people? Her gaze shot up to the doll on the dresser. It seemed too coincidental. Was someone sending her a message instead of a gift? What would happen if suddenly her doll went missing, like the picture and globe in the dollhouse? Would she disappear too? Was someone actually after her?

But why would they be?

The thought of Brad pulling up in the police car flashed through her mind. He'd walked into the house fully decked out in police gear. Of course. Maybe someone didn't like it that Brad had come over. Maybe it was a warning not to snoop.

She sighed and returned the diary to the dresser. *Or maybe it really is some weird kind of gift. Someone trying to say that I'm included in the family now. I'm Important.* She slid the drawer shut. Biting her cheek, she studied the doll again before covering it with a t-shirt. She really didn't want to look at, or think about it, again. Still, she would ask at lunch and see what Aunt Myrtle had to say.

Elise shut the bedroom door. This time though, she grabbed a stray hair from her shirt and placed it over the knob. She wanted to know the next time someone entered her room.

She looked across the hall to Anna's room and unwound another hair. Might as well keep an eye on this one, too.

# Chapter 16

Elise ran down the stairs, shaking her head at the yellow caution tape, the missing portrait, and the missing globe on the statue with its brown stain. *It's like a scene from Clue. Who know's what else is missing?*

She hurried into the dining room and stopped short. Aunt Myrtle looked up from her customary spot at the head of the table, but seated next to her was a man who looked to be in his forties. Dressed in a blue business suit and black striped tie, he leaned back in his chair to observe her. Catching her glance, he smiled.

"He came early," Aunt Myrtle quipped. "Elise, this is Stephen. Son, this is Elise, that companion your cousin hired for me."

Stephen stood up and stretched out a hand. "Hello. It's nice to meet you." Elise tried to ignore how sweaty and disheveled she felt as she shook his hand. His dark hair was swooped to the side, perfectly gelled, and expensive cologne swelled in the air. Even his pocket handkerchief was folded into a crisp point.

"Hi. How are you?" Elise asked. She smoothed the back of her head that was in disarray from her time reading the diary against the pillow, and tried to bestow an air of confidence. She'd put his age at just a few years older than her. Which meant he must have been a late surprise to Aunt Myrtle and Caroline, even more surprising.

"I'm fine. Excellent actually." His clipped words held a faint English accent. He smiled again and sat back down. Elise rounded to the other side of Aunt Myrtle and sat across from him.

"So, you are cousin Lavina's friend?" He reached for his fork and knife and cut off a piece of roast. Elise watched, fascinated as he lifted the meat up to his mouth with the fork upside down. He'd apparently adopted more than just the accent from his stay in England. "Old school chums? How quaint."

Snooty too. And, she was going to have to be nice to him. Lovely. "Err, yes." She took a sip of water to hide her expression.

Matilda came by with a salad plate for her. "Shall I skip the soup course, mum, and bring out your main course next?"

"Thank you. That'd be wonderful," Elise murmured and shook out the linen napkin across her lap. She picked up the heavy fork and cut a quick glance to Aunt Myrtle. Darn. The older woman was using a spoon in her soup.

*Screw it. Let him think I'm uncouth if he wants.* She started on her salad using the fork the way she normally did.

Stephen seemed amused by it. "It's so nice of her to hire family friends. Mother has always had a kind heart."

"What's that you say?" The older woman glowered as she looked up, her hand shaking that held the spoon. "You're talking about me like I'm not even here."

"Now, Mother, I was just saying how nice—"

"How nice I am, how nice," Aunt Myrtle interrupted. "You'll see how nice I am at the next board meeting."

Stephen paled at her words and took a sip of his wine. He set the goblet down. "Mother, you know how traveling taxes you. Tell me your ideas and I'll share them."

"Young man, I think the company's getting too big for its britches in dealing with offshore investments. I'm putting it to the vote to reel things back in. This is never what your Grandfather envisioned when he started the company. Papa would be rolling over in his grave."

Stephen snatched the glass back up and quickly drained it in a few swallows. "Mother, it's part of the future. We have to change and adapt. The small country business Grandpa designed—"

"To lend a helping hand to those in need."Aunt Myrtle interrupted sharply.

"Nowadays, we need to make money if we're going to be there to help others."

"The interest rate you're charging is disgraceful."

"If people want unsecured loans, they'll pay for it."

Aunt Myrtle's face flushed. She began to cough. Grabbing the napkin from her lap, she waved it over her face as if to get more air. Her coughing increased. Elise sprang from her chair and rushed to her side, Stephen following just a tad slower.

"Aunt Myrtle? Are you okay?"

She nodded, still coughing.

"Here, drink this." Stephen held out a cup of water. Aunt Myrtle's hand shook too hard to hold the glass, so he steadied it as she took a few sips.

"Better?" he asked.

She weakly nodded, looking deflated of all her vim and vigor that had just been on display a minute before.

"I've told you not to upset yourself. Maybe you need to go lie down?"

The old woman's shoulders rounded. She didn't look up from her soup. "Here, let me help you," her son coaxingly helped her out of the chair. He offered her his arm and handed her the cane. Together, they slowly left the dining hall.

Elise watched, feeling slightly shocked. *Poor Aunt Myrtle is really sick. Where is her daughter? I can't imagine having that kind of relationship with my mom. I love her so much, I'd want to be there if she was ill.*

Deciding to forgo her main dish, Elise headed to the kitchen hoping to make a sandwich. *Even a peanut butter and jelly would be good right about now.* Cookie was not happy to have the meal she'd prepared go uneaten but quickly cut two thick slices of homemade bread for Elise.

"Raspberry?" Cookie asked.

"That would be lovely."

"I preserved this jam myself," Cookie volunteered. She put the sandwich on a plate and poured Elise a glass of lemonade. "And this is freshly squeezed. Just like I used to do with my young 'uns," she said, passing it over.

"Thank you so much. I'm sorry again about lunch."

Cookie shrugged. "It happens. More and more of late, every time Stephen visits. She misses him, but every visit seems to take a toll on her health."

Elise took a bite and nodded. "Mmm, so good."

Cookie blushed with a happy smile. "Thank you, mum."

"So, would you say that she's getting sicker? Does her daughter come to visit?"

"No, it's only during his visits that she seems to fall ill." Licking her lip, Cookie glanced to the entrance before whispering, "And as for Caroline, not too often. Not since her father died."

Elise nodded. Picking up the plate, she thanked the cook again and headed back to her room. *At least I can finish the diary.*

Taking a drink of lemonade—*so amazing*—she looked up just in time to see Stephen walked toward the study whispering, "I've got her handled. Just give me more time."

Elise hid behind the cornice and pressed her spine against the wall.

"No! I don't want you to do that. Didn't you hear me? I told you I—" He closed the door, cutting off his last words.

At the sound of the door closing, Elise hurried for the stairs. She checked for the hair on her doorknob, but it hadn't been disturbed. Once inside, she set the plate and cup on the dresser and rubbed her forehead. That was weird. There was no denying how weird that was.

Sighing, she picked up the diary and took it to the window along with the sandwich and stood in the light to read.

*Dear Diary*

*Anna has done it again. Like a squirrel, she has gathered every person from the dollhouse. She seems to do it in her sleep, or maybe she is pretending she's sleep walking. I can't tell. Myrtle got into trouble for it today at lunch, and I couldn't allow it to go on any further. I sent Myrtle outside on assignment to gather a list of signs of Autumn from the garden and then drew Anna aside.*

*She seemed surprised when I confronted her, and vigorously shook her head adamantly. She even cried. Diary, I hardly knew what to do. She seemed so sincere. Perhaps she really was walking in her sleep. I took her to the cubby and asked her to draw the lid. She stared at it as if she'd never seen it before. When I further requested that she open it, she shook her head in denial, even going so far as to withdraw away from me. Exasperated, I pulled the lid aside.*

*Well, you can hardly imagine my shock at what I saw. Not just little people, but other things! Jewelry. Her father's good fountain pen. Dollhouse accessories. Anna shrieked and ran out of the house.*

*I fear for my job.*

*Yours,*

*Constance*

Elise shut the diary. Has this house always been a maze of deceit? What else was she going to find?

# Chapter 17

The following evening, Elise pulled into Lavina's driveway. She turned down the volume on the radio and glanced at the porch, frowning at the dark windows. *What the heck, Lavina? Your car is here. Where are you?* Normally, Lavina's house was lit up enough to threaten a town brown-out.

Elise shifted the car into park and glanced at her watch. Just fifteen minutes until class started. Swallowing hard, she tried to ignore the butterflies freaking out in her stomach. *You better be here, Lavina, and not off with Mr. G. somewhere.*

The car door sounded overly loud when she shut it as she went to knock on the door. *Why the heck am I freaking out about this? It's just a defense class.* She started to pound on the door.

Her fist hadn't hit the door twice before it swung open, showing a very cheerful Lavina. Clad head to toe in ridiculous yoga gear—a sport's bra halter and painted on pants—with her red curls pulled away from her face, she said, "You about took my front door off. What are you all in a stir for?" Lavina pushed her out of the way and locked the door.

"I was sure you were asleep." Elise grumbled. "Or out with Mr. G."

"Asleep? Why on earth would I be asleep?" Lavina walked briskly ahead, her new white tennis shoes squeaking from not having a chance to be broken in. "Now no more shimmy-shammying. Get in. We're going to be late."

Elise blinked hard at the quick turn of events, almost disappointed that Lavina was ready. It had been in the back of her mind to not go if her friend couldn't make it. Elise blew out a breath and hurried to the driver's side.

Lavina dropped into the passenger seat, bringing a heavy scent of lavender and rose with her. "All right. Let's go." She brushed her red hair off her shoulder.

"Seatbelt," Elise directed, hand hovering with the key over the ignition.

Lavina rolled her eyes and snapped the seatbelt into place. She stretched out her legs looking to get comfortable and adjusted the belt across her chest. "Seatbelt doesn't work for a woman as well-endowed as I am, you know."

Elise snorted. "Lavina, you've been using that excuse since you were ten years old. Just wear it and shut up about it."

"Whatever you say. Now can we go?" She looked at her nails. "Just to warn you, I may be more of a watcher than a participator. I just had a manicure, you know."

"Where's all your big talk about beating men?"

Lavina smiled slyly, her eyeliner perfectly winged. "Depends on how good-looking the man is."

Elise turned up the hill that led into town. The Pinto shuddered for a moment before gearing down.

Lavina frowned. "Is this thing okay?"

"It's fine. Not every car is like your Camaro."

"Watch out for that pop can," Lavina shrieked in fake alarm, pointing straight ahead.

"Whatever." Out of spite, Elise purposely aimed for the aluminum can and ran it over.

"My gosh, woman. So daring. You must have a death wish." Lavina's eyes were huge, before she leaned back with a sarcastic grin.

"Very funny, Lavina. But if you want to talk death wishes, what the heck did you get me into out there at Montgomery Manor?"

"I did warn you that she was my crazy aunt."

"I don't recall too much of a warning, more like begging that she had to have a companion. And that you didn't want to do it."

Lavina's green eyes narrowed. "I'm sure I told you she was crazy."

Elise shrugged. "Well, crazy or not, something really strange is going on up there." With the throttle to the floor, she mentally coaxed her car. *Come on. You can do it! Don't embarrass me and bog out now.*

"More than dead bodies?" Lavina asked.

"Uh," Elise darted a look toward her friend. Lavina rubbed her temple as though a headache were starting. "Yes."

"Like what?"

"How often did you visit your Aunt Myrtle?"

"Christmas and Easter. Aunt Myrtle didn't hold to any Sunday dinner gatherings."

"Did you ever hang out with your cousins?"

"Oh, do you mean Stephen? That man acted like he was the king gator in a goldfish pond. Always bragging. I could hardly stand to be around him. Always teased me for living in a rattrap of a house."

"Well, the Manor might have some rat problems now. Aunt Myrtle still thinks there is a ghost."

Lavina stared at her askance. "Even after the police told her it was the derelict?"

"Yeah, she says she still hears it. And it's not just her," Elise continued hurriedly. "Although they don't come straight out and say it, so does the help. I'm kind of freaked out."

"Elise, you can't believe the ramblings of an old woman and her compliant staff. Honestly...."

"I'm telling you, I've heard weird stuff at night myself, and seen things disappear."

"Elise, are you serious? Do you hear how you sound?"

Elise sighed. "I know, I know. It sounds crazy."

Lavina stared at her a second longer. "You okay? Maybe this job was too much after the whole cruise ship debacle."

Elise braked at the stop light. "Honestly, Lavina. Do I look loony to you? Anyway, speaking of cruises, when is your next one? Surely Mr. G is about to whisk you away again."

"Oh, he's got some plans," Lavina laughed. "But I don't want to make you jealous. Poor thing."

"Poor thing? You still on me for not having a man?"

Lavina shrugged.

"Well, you'll be happy to know that Brad and I are dating."

Her friend gasped. "What? And you didn't tell me?"

"What do you mean? I'm telling you."

"Well done, little Padawan, well done." Lavina smiled. "So, is this what the self-defense is all about? To impress Brad?"

"Uh, definitely not." Elise shook her head. She bit her cheek to hide her irritation.

"I'm just checking. You've come so far. I don't want you to fall back into your old ways like you did with Mark."

"Nope. Never again. I'm staying faithful to me first. I'm doing this because I really do want to grow. And I think it actually might be a good thing to know."

"I can't argue with that. Especially with your knack for discovering dead bodies."

Elise turned the corner and pulled into the lot of the strip mall and parked. Listed on one of the building fronts was the name, Safety First. Nerves crawled over her and she blew out a deep breath to steady herself. She looked over at Lavina. "You ready?"

Lavina plucked out her lipstick from her purse and pulled down the sun visor for the mirror. Quickly, she reapplied a thin coat before turning to Elise. "I was born ready. Let's go."

They walked inside the building. Elise's legs felt like they were made of water and she willed herself not to shake. The bright overhead lights blared from the ceiling, competing with the red and blue rubber mats for the senses.

Elise swallowed hard and Lavina gave her a soft nudge. "I think the rest of our class is over there." She indicated with a nod of her red head.

The two women joined a group of six others that stood against the wall. There was an older woman with a younger one—Elise overheard the younger one say, "mom"—three college-aged looking women, and another older woman who appeared to be in her late sixties. Standing in front of them was a man dressed in black sweats. His sweatshirt was emblazoned in white with the words *Safety First*. He turned and gave them an easy smile as they approached. "Newcomers! Glad you made it." He walked over with his hand out. "Hi. I'm Dave."

Just having him approach, knowing what the class was about, knowing this was the man she'd eventually have to yell at and practice defense moves against, made Elise's heart pound. The palms of her hands felt sweaty as she reached for his. She managed a weak grin. "Hi, I'm Elise."

He tipped his head. "Elise…."

"Pepper."

His eyebrows flickered. "Are you…." He smiled and shook his head. "You aren't that companion that Myrtle Kennington has now, are you?"

Elise felt a poke of shock. "Yeah, I am. How did you know?"

He grinned sheepishly. "I live there. That is, I throw down a bed roll at my dad's, when I'm not sleeping here." He pointed above him. "There's a little studio upstairs."

Lavina butted in. "And you sleep at Aunt Myrtle's where?"

His mouth opened. "Oh, hey. Aunt Myrtle huh? Wow, this is a small world. My granddad is her chauffeur." He grinned again, the grin of someone who knew he was good looking.

Lavina gave him a cold measuring glance. "Ernest is your grandpa?"

When he smiled back his eyes crinkled. "It seems like everybody's related up on that hill. Hey, I remember you. Tiny little thing with red pigtails. We played out in the woods once. Maybe doctor or something." He winked.

"I assure you, it wasn't doctor. I only play that with actual doctors." Lavina raised an eyebrow before walking away.

"Geez, was it something I said?" he muttered, watching her talk with the group of young women.

"She's going to let you have it," Elise warned. "Maybe next time, don't bring up playing doctor before teaching a person how to whale on you."

He rubbed the back of his neck and looked down chuckling. "Me and my big mouth. Well, come on. Join the rest of the class."

# Chapter 18

Elise woke the next morning at seven. She covered her face and groaned. *I'm so not a morning person. My brain feels like oatmeal.* She toyed with the idea of going back to sleep.

The class had ended the night before with Lavina never once addressing the instructor again. She did, however, give him a sharp kick to the groin that he seemed to feel, from the purple look on his face, despite all of his protective clothing.

Elise smiled at the memory. It had actually been a lot easier than she expected, especially with all the other women, who seemed just as nervous as she was. Together, they supported each other, all of them cheering the person on who had to yell and defend against the attacker. They'd even had to defend against a knife attack— albeit a rubber one—blocking a left thrust.

The only real scary moment was when Dave acted out a scene as a sleazy-talking stalker trying to overpower her outside a pretend parking lot. Elise had wanted to freeze up but her support team rallied her through. The instructor had looked slightly discomforted when the women began chanting, "Kill! Kill! Kill!" Elise practiced all the moves against him that she'd just been taught and ran away.

The cheers of "Yeah, Elise! Let him have it! You go girl!" still rang in her ears.

Turns out, she could do a lot more things than she ever thought.

When they'd left the class, Dave handed out business cards, which Lavina deemed to ignore. Awkwardly, he passed them to Elise. "Tell your friends to join. Heck, tell strangers. Everyone should take a safety course, and I'm a little desperate for customers. I also do personal training." He lowered his chin and winked at Elise with those last words, taking her off guard. At that angle, Elise thought he looked familiar. She took the business cards gingerly as if they were covered in slug slime.

They were now sitting on the dresser. *And I'm throwing them out just as soon as I get out of this bed.* She rolled over and looked out the window. The trees weren't blowing, a good sign that it might be sunny today. *Hey. It's been a while since I've checked the dollhouse. What if something new is missing? How would I ever know?*

*Get up, get up, get up.* Grumbling to herself, she climbed out of the warm covers. *I've got a job to do. I have to find out what's going on here. I owe it to Aunt Myrtle and Lavina both to figure it out.*

Elise got herself ready for the day, then steeled herself to go check on the dollhouse.

She darted across the hall to Anna's old room.

The dollhouse stood shielded in shadows. Even though it was morning, the room was still dark on this side of the house. She flipped on the lamp and walked over to the dollhouse. First, she checked the replica of Myrtle's childhood bedroom, half afraid that there would be a miniature doll of herself on the bed. The bed was clear, and she breathed a sigh of relief, feeling free to relax and study the house more.

Myrtle's tiny room was cute. There were a few things that were changed. Of course, there was the dollhouse sitting in the corner, on the bureau. A different quilt was on the bed. And, she realized for the first time, there was a desk in the corner.

On the far wall, the room had a little white door. Heaviness grew in her belly. She knew where the door led, to the room's attached bathroom. At that moment, Elise realized that every time she'd examined the house, she'd never looked in that bathroom. But she knew why she'd been so reluctant. She didn't want to see the mini replica of the room the gardener had died in. *Come on, now. Just take a quick peek.* With a deep breath, she studied the bathroom.

It was a cute little bathroom, but her senses gave a twinge right away. Something seemed off, missing maybe? She looked again, trying to figure out what it was. Toilet. Sink with a vanity. A tub. The vanity held a tiny cup with a toothbrush and a comb.

Still, something was definitely absent.

It bothered her but she couldn't find it. Frustrated, she moved on to the next room, another bedroom. This one seemed sterile of any personal touch, and Elise assumed it was a guest bedroom. There were four more in a row before the hall ended.

The opposite side of the house held the rooms on the other side of the hall. More guest bedrooms with Anna's room and the enormous master bedroom as bookends.

She looked into Anna's bathroom for a clue as to what might be different in the other.

It was identical to the first. Even the window had the same tiny curtains.

Elise looked at the counter with its cup and toothbrush and finally realized what was missing.

She pushed away as reluctance grew in a ball in her stomach. There was nothing for it. The only way to find out was to go check and see if it was true.

Biting the inside of her cheek, Elise slid her phone from her pocket. *I just want to call Brad and have him keep me phone company.* She wrinkled her nose. *How is this going to sound? "Hello, Brad. I'm too scared to go to the bathroom. Can you drop what you're doing in training and stay with me on the phone?"*

She dialed him anyway. *He's always up for a good laugh.*

"So, what are you up to?" she asked when Brad answered.

"Flipping through the channels. You?" His sarcastic tone made her laugh, knowing how her response was going to shake him up.

"What are you really doing?"

"You caught me on my fifteen minute break. I've just finished a six mile run." He didn't even sound out of breath.

"Six miles? It's only seven in the morning."

"They get us up at five around here. And the day is just beginning." Brad sounded slightly glum.

"I'm never complaining again."

He snorted. "Alright. What's going on? I know it has to be important."

"Mmm, I think I found another clue." *Wait for it. Wait for it.*

"Dear Lord. What now?"

"It's probably nothing," Elise assured him. "I'm sure it's nothing. But I did find something new missing in the dollhouse and I'm just going to take a sec and check it out."

"Check where?"

"The bathroom." Elise waited a beat before dropping, "where the gardener was murdered."

A sharp exhale came from the receiver. "Don't do anything yet. Let me call my buddy to swing by."

"What? Don't be silly. It's just across the hall."

"Elise…."

"I just want you to keep me company, is all. Because it's kind of spooky. Can you stay on the line?"

She left Anna's bedroom and walked over to the one she'd originally been given. *It's probably nothing. How on earth could they take it anyway? And why?*

"You in there yet?" he growled. "You're killing me here, Elise."

"Almost," she whispered and opened the door.

The interior gloom was cut by a crack of light seeping from the edge of the curtain. The room itself smelled stale and unused, with a faint metallic scent that hung in the air.

*That can't be blood. It has to be my imagination.*

Swallowing hard, she used her cell to light the way to the bathroom.

"There yet?" Brad's voice made her jump.

"I'll tell you when I'm there!" she answered irritably.

"Don't be grumpy with me. Hanging here waiting for you is way worse than the six mile run."

Elise flung the door open and flashed the beam over to the sink. Disappointment flooded her, and she muttered, "Shoot."

"What's the matter?"

"The mirror had been missing in the dollhouse. But, it's here in the bathroom."

Brad was quiet. Elise began again, half embarrassed. "You don't suppose...."

"What?"

"I mean, *it's* crazy, but I've seen it done in murder movies."

"*You're* driving me crazy. What?"

Elise bit her bottom lip, hesitating just for a moment. Her gaze darted over to the shower. In a second she was over there turning the hot water on full blast. She flipped the shower lever.

"Lawd, woman. You going to tell me, or continue to make me crazy?"

"Just give me a second." The room slowly filled with steam. She crossed back across the room and shut the door.

When she turned to look at the mirror, chills of excitement ran up her back. *Holy cow. There it was.* "You're not going to believe it...."

"I believe it," Brad said dryly. "Just tell me."

She didn't need to turn on the bathroom's overhead. She could see by the light of the little window.

Showing up on the mirror from the steam were the words, "Pay or You're next." She read them out loud to

Brad and gave a tiny giggle. "I can't believe that worked!"

"You're reading a death threat and laughing."

The giggle froze in her throat. "Oh, my gosh. You're right."

"Yeah, this puts the murder in a whole new light. I don't know who that threat is for. It could even be for you. I don't like you there at all."

"This means it might not have been that derelict." Elise turned off the water.

"Kind of makes that motive go down the toilet. What kind of derelict would leave a threat for someone else?"

"And go through the trouble of removing the mirror in the dollhouse?"

"Exactly. It has to be someone in the house. Someone you know."

Elise rubbed her temple and spun back for her bedroom. "I'm not sure what I'm going to do." She shut the door and wandered over to the window. The sun was just peeking over the hill and lighting the remaining red and gold leaves on the trees like embers.

"How about get out." Brad was blunt and to the point as usual.

"No, Aunt Myrtle needs me. I'll be okay. I'm taking that safety class, you know."

Brad groaned. "That safety class isn't something that can keep you safe in the middle of a viper's nest. Don't let it give you a false sense of security. It's an emergency tactic to get out. And right now, you can just get out."

"I can't, Brad. I have a job to do. I can't leave Aunt Myrtle right now. But I promise I won't do anything stupid."

The bell rang, signaling breakfast. "Brad, I have to go. It's time for breakfast."

There was a sarcastic cough. "Seriously? How can you eat at a time like this?"

"Oh, you don't know Aunt Myrtle. I don't dare go against her, again. Meals are prompt, and so far I've avoided any consequences for being late."

"Yeah, well, that's fine. Leave me here to worry about you."

"Awww, you're worried about me?" Elise teased.

"It's not funny."

"Don't worry. Seriously. You have to take care of yourself, too. Maybe I'll talk Lavina into spending the night."

"That would help me feel better. At least, until I can get forensics in there to look at the mirror. They should be there later today, so stick around. And, whatever you do, don't tell anyone about it."

"You've got it."

"Call me tonight?"

"Call? Not text? You really must be worried."

"I miss you. Can't wait to get back."

"Me either." She felt a little prickle of anxiety as she glanced at her watch again. "But I have to go."

"Yeah. Yeah. Old lady with a cane. You're scared of her but not a murderer. I got it."

She laughed and hung up.

*Wow, I'm laughing. Brad can cheer me up no matter what's going on in my life. Man, that's saying something.*

The ancient phone on her nightstand rang, sounding like the rusty cry of a cat in heat. Elise glanced at it, half in disbelief and half in humor. *Okay, then. I guess the housekeepers are getting used to me living here. No more five-star treatment of knocking at my door with a polite "mum". They're using the 'new technology.'* She laughed at the second ring, picturing an anxious Cookie on the other end, and picked up the phone. "Hello?"

"Miss Pepper?" the male voice was muffled.

"Yes?"

"You like your new toy?"

"My new..."

"Her hair made me smile every time I brushed it."

Elise's mouth went dry as her gaze darted to the dresser. The doll was gone.

"See how easy it is to reach you?" the voice continued. "You're always so alone. So nosy, but so alone."

"Who are you?" Elise inserted anger into her voice. *Never let them see you afraid.*

"Oh, you're tough." A low laugh. "I know you're afraid. And, I haven't even touched you yet."

"Listen you sicko—" The sharp click of him hanging up interrupted her.

She squeezed the receiver in frustration. Someone was watching her. Someone knew when she was in her room, and when she left. She had to be more careful.

But in a way, she was relieved. Because the voice sure didn't sound ghostly.

*Do I call Brad back?* Elise shook her head. *He'll leave his training and swoop in like a knight in shining armor. Maybe I'll tell Lavina at class today.* She wrinkled her nose. *You know how she gets when she worries. And then I get blamed for her eating a quart of ice cream.*

A wave of heaviness drooped over her. *I know what I need, my cat. That's settled, I'm going home for a bit.*

She took the stairs two at a time and heard voices down the hall. Who was that? It couldn't be. Aunt Myrtle laughing? She sidled down the hall toward the dining room. On her way, she heard raspy male laughter. She snuck a peek around the corner.

Apparently, she wasn't the only one to miss breakfast. Stephen was notably missing, too. But who *was* there was Uncle Shorty, who sat grinning delightfully at Aunt Myrtle as she talked.

"And, if you can believe, that rooster was back at it the very next day!" Aunt Myrtle finished her story, before giving Uncle Shorty a sly grin.

He threw his head up and laughed. "Myrtle, you've always known how to tell a story."

Aunt Myrtle smiled back. "And you've always known how to be the best audience."

He winked at her. "Come on, Myrtle, you know you've always wanted to marry me. Let's go do it. Think of the statement we'd make by finally combining our estates."

"Oh, you old coot. You never change."

Smiling, Elise tiptoed away, hoping they hadn't seen her. *I guess I won't have to excuse myself from breakfast after all. I bet she won't even notice I'm gone.*

She stopped short. It was still quite early. How long had Uncle Shorty been there? Every time something weird had happened, he'd been around. Was he somehow trying to scare Aunt Myrtle into marrying him so he could have the property?

Shaking her head, she hurried for the front door. *That sweet old man? I'm thinking crazy.* She jogged to her car and climbed into the driver's seat. As she turned the ignition, common sense gave her a knock on the head. *How crazy can you think when you're getting threatening phone calls? Tread lightly and watch everything. Everyone's a suspect at this point.*

Elise drove down the hill past the other mansions forgotten in time. All the times she'd gone back and forth to town, she'd never seen any signs of life. *Weird. If I lived in any of these, I'd have huge parties. Or horses. Or adopt animals. Or something! Such a waste of space.*

Her house looked a little forlorn when she pulled in the driveway, too.

"I haven't forgotten you," she said looking up at the little cottage. *I love this place.* Her fingers trailed against the white railing of the porch as she went up the stairs. She took in her cute white wicker chairs and pink petunia plant and felt a strong stab of homesickness. She unlocked the front door and whistled lightly for her cat. He'd gone running off in a huff when she'd let him inside last night, so it filled her with joy to see him come scrambling out from the bedroom. "Hey, sweetheart." Max sat a few feet away watching her. "Are you still mad at me? I'll be home soon for good." She cleaned his water bowl and refilled it, then opened a can of cat food.

Taking them outside, she placed the dishes on the porch and sat on the step. Max jogged over, his belly swinging. "You're such a big boy. I've missed you so much." He butted his head against her leg. All was forgiven.

"Sweet boy. But someone has to pay for the cat food. And look at it this way, you get the whole house to yourself at night. Even the top of the buffet."

Max purred in response. She scratched his ears before trying to haul him into her lap. His front end stretched while his back end remained firmly planted on the step. "Fine. stay there then." She set him back down and he wiped his cheek on her arm. "Am I your girl?" she whispered, leaning over to kiss his head.

He sat on the step with his tail doing lazy sweeps. While her fingers continued to run through his fur, she gazed out into the yard.

It was beautiful here. No mansion by any expanse of the imagination, but she had her own little paradise. Max's body rumbled under her hand as he purred. *And, my own rescued friend. Although, who rescued whom is hard to say.*

*What is going up at the Manor? Why would someone threaten me to back off? It's been a while since Brad came over. What did I do that they didn't like?*

Stephen's snooty face flashed through her mind. *He doesn't like me. Why? Does he want his mom to be alone and scared? What the heck is his problem?*

"Honestly, I'd be done with this job. But no way am I giving up." Her words reminded her of what Charlotte had said. Apparently, Manchester Manor drove everyone to want to quit.

"Alright, Max. I think I have to go back and do some more searching. This all has to be connected to the gardener's death, somehow in a way that makes sense. I'm missing something. I just don't know what it is yet." Max stood with his front paws on her knee and stretched to sniff her face. Elise smiled at the tickle of his whiskers.

"And later, I have self-defense class where I get to yell at the instructor." Max blinked green eyes at her. "Yes, it's just that impressive. But I'll see you tonight, okay? It's going to be me instead of Brad because he has a dumb class, so don't be disappointed. Be a good boy."

With a final scratch on the cat's head, she got up and climbed into her car.

# Chapter 19

Elise pulled up to the house, noting that Uncle Shorty's motorcycle was gone. *Alright. I've regrouped. I can figure this thing out. There has to be a clue in that room as to who is doing this.* She slammed the car door and hurried up the steps.

Hamilton opened the door for her. He looked every bit as professional as ever.

"Good morning," she said cheerfully.

"Good morning, Ms. Pepper. It appears it will be clear and sunny today."

"My favorite kind of weather." Elise shrugged out of her coat and draped it over one arm. "Hamilton, I'm glad you're here because I've been meaning to ask you something. Have you seen anything weird going on around here?"

He raised a bushy eyebrow at her. "Weird, ma'am?"

Elise hedged and tried again. "You know, like things disappearing? Aunt Myrtle thinks the place is haunted by her sister." She glanced up at him. "What do you think?"

Hamilton looked down his beak-like nose. "Her sister's been gone more than sixty years, ma'am. Ms. Kennington misses her terribly, so it's natural in those circumstances to entertain some fanciful thinking. This house is old, and does strange things. Perhaps Ms. Kennington is in search of comfort is reading this as signs from another world." He slowly blinked, clearly done with this type of talk.

Elise cleared her throat. "Of course, you're right. It's easy to get caught up in the talk around her."

"You are being paid, I believe, to be a support to her. Not to encourage her to pursue make-believe stories." His words were cold and abrupt.

Elise pressed her lips together, trying to contain herself. "Naturally, my role is to support her however I can. She misses her children. Surely you know what that feels like." Then, a flicker of doubt crossed her mind. "Do you have children, Hamilton?"

"I proudly devoted my life to my job, and I consider the Kenningtons as my family."

Elise nodded. "They are lucky to have you. Do you have any other family around?"

He straightened his shoulders. "The last of my family just recently died, ma'am. Now, will there be anything else?"

Elise inwardly cringed at his words. *Can I put my foot further in my mouth?* "No, that's all. Thank you."

She left him at the doorway and climbed the stairs to her room. As she passed the missing portrait she decided to check on Anna's room instead. Maybe just being in there would spark some type of insight as to what was going on.

Once again, the room was dark and gloomy. Elise turned on the lamp and sank to the bed to stare at the dollhouse. Who was taking these things and why? Her thoughts flittered with the idea of Anna, but her mind refused to accept the explanation of a ghost. *It can't be Anna. For one thing, why on earth would a ghost want a blue marble or a mirror?*

*Maybe to match the chair she once took.* She shook her head. *Ridiculous.*

*Right. Ridiculous. About as crazy as the maid ending up with shoes two different sizes and a dead man leaving a message on the bathroom mirror.*

She flopped back on the bed and coughed at the dust. *I feel like I just got smacked with the puff of grandma's face powder.*

*Why can't I figure this out? I'm an intelligent woman being run around by ghosts.*

Her gaze traveled around the room, stopping on the bookshelf. The top shelf held many duplicates of the same books that were downstairs in the library.

The next shelf held encyclopedias and the one below that bible stories. The bottom shelf grabbed her attention because the books had been haphazardly shoved in a row with no attention paid to their different sizes. She leaned forward. They weren't in alphabetical order either. One of the books had fallen to its side with a few more tilting in the same direction.

Something about that rubbed her the wrong way. *Why would every other shelf be so neat and tidy and this one left in chaos?* She got to her feet and walked over. Kneeling down, she reached and pushed the books back upright, examining the titles. The books were fiction, and nonfiction alike, quite an eclectic assortment. *Maybe that was why they in there with such lack of care.*

Elise started to get up when something else caught her attention. The back of the shelf didn't seem to properly line up with the side, and a black crack showed in one corner. She touched the crack and felt movement.

The back of the bottom shelf fell off with a clatter. Her mouth dropped as several of the books fell into the open space. Still kneeling, she gathered the books off the shelf and stacked them in a tower against the wall. Then, she scooted down on her belly and directed her cell's flashlight into the space.

It seemed to open up into a hidden room. Excitement flooded through her. She cast a quick look behind to be sure the door was shut and wiggled her way through.

Dirt scraped her belly as she pushed in to the other side. She kicked her legs and twisted her way in. The space was narrow but proved to be tall enough for her to stand.

She rose to her feet and brushed off her front while shining the light with her other hand.

The space was the cavity between the interior bedroom walls and the exterior walls. *It had to have been made on purpose. But why?* Horizontal lines of lathe dripped with gray plaster that had been applied to the other side. Every inch of the space was grimy with dust.

*What is that? Glimmering in the corner?* She flashed her light on it and silver sparkled back. Something was stuck under the crevice of the wall. She reached for it. Stuck.

Sitting back on her heels, she studied it. Whatever it was, it was metallic and wedged tight. *Maybe my license would fit under there? A credit card? Even a bobby pin would work.* But that would involve going back to her room, and she wasn't ready to leave yet. She looked at her shoelace and rolled the plastic tip in her fingers. *Hmm.* She slipped the shoe off and tried to fit the lace under the crack.

It just fit. She dragged the tip along the edge of the silver thing, managing to pry the object out just enough to grab it with her fingernails.

A silver coin. She held it under the light and read the words "Freedom dollar" in script under the picture of Liberty. Stamped in tiny letters was the date 1926.

Freedom dollar. She'd heard that before, but from where? She turned it over and examined the back, running a fingernail along the ridged edge. Although tarnished, it was in pristine condition. She tucked the coin into her pocket and shone the light down the rest of the passage, noting the wall scaffolding of the next room. If she turned sideways, she could just squeeze along the corridor. She hesitated, the beam of light bouncing off of dust, cobwebs, and chunks of fallen plaster. *Do I really want to go down there?*

She sighed. Of course she did, in a weird love/hate way. How could she stop now? Taking a couple deep breaths to pump herself up, she eyed the cobwebs. *I'm the bravest chicken there ever was.*

Cautiously, she stepped into the narrow space. Her heart jumped into her throat as her foot rolled across a piece of rubble and she nearly fell. *Careful.* She glanced at the lathe. *If you fall, you'll go right through that wall.* She snickered at the thought. *Surprise!*

She nearly fell again. *Okay, be serious now.*

Elise reached to pull down the cobweb then wiped her hand quickly on the back of her pants. Trying to keep good footing, she edged forward.

The crawl-way was pitch-black except for what she could see by her cell. Dust sifted down from above. Elise held her breath but it was too late. She could feel the tickle in her lungs. *Don't cough. Whatever you do. Do not cough.* The tickling got stronger, and desperately, she hid her mouth in the crook of her arm and gently cleared her throat. Slowly, she took a deep breath in, and blew it out.

The sensation subsided.

She moved forward again, running the light down the wall. *What's the point of this space? Are there peepholes?* Other than the old gray webs and dust, she didn't see anything of interest. *Wait, what was that? Maybe?* Maybe there was a bit of dust knocked off from the wall joist right there. As if someone fell forward.... Elise took a step and leaned as if she were falling, trying to see where her hand lined up. The mark was just above where her hand would have fallen. Someone taller than her then? A man?

Or maybe nothing.

She flashed the light on the floor looking for footsteps.

The floor didn't show any, but that didn't mean anything. A quick glance behind her proved void of her own footsteps.

She flipped the light ahead and saw that the pathway ended abruptly with a wall.

There was a faint glimmer in the expanse of black. She sidled closer.

A hairline crack near the bottom allowed light from whatever was on the other side of the wall to shine through. She examined the wall, expecting lathe and plaster, but instead saw solid wood. *Oh, my gosh. That crack continues all the way around. This must be the back of another bookcase.*

She squatted down and peered through the gap. Everything on the other side appeared as a pink explosion until her eyes could focus. A pair of pink drapes covered French doors. There was a pink, puffy comforter. Aunt Myrtle lay still on the bed. Elise jerked away, thinking hard. *What in the world? A direct passage from Anna's room to her parents? Did they know?*

*Was this passage meant to be here the whole time?*

"I hear you! Go away. You go away now!"

Elise nearly screamed at the voice. Licking her lip, she peeped through the crack again. Aunt Myrtle sat looking in her direction, making Elise's blood run cold. "I said I was sorry, Anna! You leave me alone!"

Elise backed away from the wall, her heart hammering. *What is going on here?* Was this what Myrtle had been hearing all along? Was somebody torturing this poor woman, using her guilty memories as a sharp sword? Frowning, Elise made her way back to the other room as quietly as possible.

Once out of the passage, she shimmied the book shelf until it fastened shut. Her knees were covered in dust and her hands felt grimy. She brushed them off, grimacing. Her emotions didn't feel any better.

She replaced the books. *Did Anna once do this? Take the books out and creep down there? Why? Was there somehow a way outside?*

With a frustrated sigh, she turned off the light and hurried back to her room. *The diary. I need to finish it. The secret has to be in there somewhere.* It occurred to her how curious it was that Constance wrote more about Anna than she did about Myrtle. Anna seemed to have been a puzzle for everyone.

She locked her bedroom door and opened the diary, walking to the window to read by the light.

*Dear Diary.*

*Myrtle is such a joy, but such a challenge to her mother. I hardly know how to help the poor girl because all she wants to do is run, play and laugh. Her mother constantly scolds her to be silent. I've begun to take her to the back part of the woods, where she meets a family friend. Mrs. Montgomery would be furious, but how can I refuse?*

*The other day, I asked Myrtle what she thought about the missing dollhouse pieces. The poor girl blushed and looked miserable. It took me promising her that I'd let her visit Thomas (whom she calls Shorty, although I've admonished her several times that it isn't lady-like). She's finally confessed that her sister is playing a game and the dollhouse pieces are clues to her game. I asked her how to play it, but that's all she would say on the matter.*

*Yours*

*Constance*

*Dear Diary,*

*Today, I noticed Anna skulking and decided to follow her, thinking she had stolen something again. She surprised me. I think she might have a beau. A young man met her. They held hands before she looked over her shoulder. Her mother would be furious if she knew. I darted behind the pyramidal hedge to avoid being seen, and when I looked again, they were gone inside the maze. I feel like I've seen him before, so I'll have to watch more carefully. I think he may be one who accompanies the milkman.*

*Yours,*

*Constance*

The lunch bell dinged. Elise felt a twitch of irritation at being interrupted and returned the thread before sticking the diary back in the drawer of her dresser.

# Chapter 20

Elise headed down to the dining room for lunch, her muscles tensing at the thought of seeing Aunt Myrtle. She wasn't sure how she'd respond if Aunt Myrtle brought up what she'd heard in her room. Just thinking about it gave Elise the strangest sensation of heaviness and excitement all twisted together.

The older woman did seem to be pensive when Elise arrived. She stirred her tea over and over, seemingly mindless of the tink-tink-tink the spoon made against the sides of the china cup.

Stephen sat next to his mother scrolling through his cell and typing furiously. "Hi," he said, with a quick glance as Elise settled in across from him. Elise found it curious that he wore a business shirt and tie on what was supposed to be a vacation.

"Hello," she answered back, including Aunt Myrtle with a nod. Aunt Myrtle ignored her, focusing instead with a blank stare out the window.

Charlotte served lunch, but still Aunt Myrtle stirred her tea.

"Stephen, do you remember playing with Papa?" Aunt Myrtle said suddenly, startling Elise. Stephen raised his head up from his phone looking just as surprised.

He cleared his throat. "Yes, of course I do."

Aunt Myrtle laughed, but the emotion didn't carry up to her eyes, which were shadowed in sadness. "Do you remember how you two used to play pirates? With real treasure?"

"Yes," he smiled. "It would be nice to have some of those coins now. Just one would bring in ten thousand dollars in today's market."

"Oh, that wasn't even a quarter of what he had." Tink. Tink. Tink. The spoon made its endless trip around the cup.

"Mother, what's gotten into you?" Stephen's forehead wrinkled in concern. "Are you having one of your spells?"

"Did I ever tell you what happened to Anna?" She set the spoon down and finally looked at Elise.

Stephen groaned and rubbed the back of his neck. "Mother...."

Aunt Myrtle ignored him. "There was a cave she used to go to, about halfway up the side of a cliff. Someone had rigged a rope bridge between the top of this old maple tree and a boulder that was on the other side. I wanted to go there so bad, but Anna wouldn't let me. I was a booger and went right home and told Papa. I was still mad about getting into trouble for the dollhouse furniture."

"Mother, don't go there. Don't do this to yourself."

"You hush now, boy. Let me finish."

Stephen rolled his eyes and slumped back in the chair.

Aunt Myrtle stared at her bony hands folded in her lap. "You know, I knew I shouldn't tattle. Later, I wished I hadn't. It was one of those moments that the second those words left my mouth, I knew I'd done something bad. That I'd changed everything. Well, I've never seen Papa so angry. He took one of our uncles and another neighbor and went out there and they tore that rope bridge down. Anna was furious with me and said she'd never forgive me."

Elise could almost see the heaviness of that memory weighing down on the little woman. Aunt Myrtle's shoulders bowed more. The old woman continued in a low voice. "I was crushed, but then, there was nothing I could do about it. I just hoped one day my sister would forget." She looked up. "But Anna never forgets."

Elise jerked at the present tense verb. She shifted and crossed her legs on the other side, propping her chin on her hand.

Aunt Myrtle sighed. "Then one day I saw her run across the lawn. I followed her. I followed Anna. She climbed up the tree and headed out on a branch, just staring at the cave. I couldn't help myself and begged her to stop. When she saw me, she screamed and told me to go home. And then her foot slipped. I saw it happen." Her bottom lip trembled and eyes filled with tears as she looked desperately at Elise. "It was my fault she died."

Elise blinked, feeling tears in her own eyes. She reached for Aunt Myrtle's hand and grabbed it. "It wasn't your fault. It was in no way your fault."

"You don't know, you...." Aunt Myrtle whispered as tears cut tracks down her wrinkled cheeks. She sniffed and pulled her hand away to reach for her napkin and wiped her cheek.

Stephen leaned back in his chair with his eyes shut. "Mother, let it go. You've been beating yourself up for that for years. What's done is done. No matter how sad you are, you can't bring her back."

Shock flooded through Elise at the coldness of his words. Aunt Myrtle's face stiffened and all emotions fell away. She took a sip of her tea. "You're quite right, Stephen. Thank you."

Stephen appeared relieved at the turn of his mother's response. He picked up a fork and poked at the turkey meat before him. "Turkey, eh?"

"Don't you worry. Tonight, we're having prime rib for your birthday."

"Mother, I'm not going to be here tonight. I told you I was going out."

"Stephen, I've had it all planned. We'll have an early dinner." The old woman looked at him beseechingly.

Either the earlier story or the look softened him and he sighed. "Fine, as long as I can leave by seven."

Aunt Myrtle smiled, and the years seemed to roll back from her face. "Good. I'll let Cookie know." She cut off a sliver of the meat and brought it to her mouth.

After the latest story of Anna, Elise was itching to get through lunch and back to the diary. Would it mention the hidden room or Anna's death? She ate as quickly as possible, feeling like a little kid rushing to go outside and play. Leaving the last few bites, she wiped her mouth. "Lovely lunch. I have a few things to do so I'm going to run," she excused herself.

Stephen watched her leave with a flicker of interest in his eyes.

Elise hurried up the stairwell, unable to stop from cringing at the bare spot on the wall. Secrets. Secrets everywhere. She shut the bedroom door behind her, then rushed to the dresser for the diary. Before she even got to her bed, she'd flipped it open and was reading.

*Dear Diary,*

*This is such a sad day, I hardly know what to write. Anna has gone home to be with her maker. Mrs. Montgomery threatened to join Anna and nearly threw herself from the turret window, had not Mr. Montgomery been there to stop her. Poor Mr. Montgomery has been beside himself and we could all hear him begging her to be strong.*

*I haven't seen Myrtle all day, and so I'm going out to search. In the meantime, I'm hiding this behind the brick until I have more time. I don't dare chance anyone finding it.*

Elise flipped through the rest of the pages, but there wasn't anymore entries. She shut the book with a frown. Constance had been sent home the very next day as the family shut down with grief, leaving poor Myrtle to mourn not one, but two of her most constant companions.

Something about the last entry troubled her. Elise opened it to reread, pausing on the words, "behind the brick." What brick? There wasn't a brick in front of the hiding spot in Myrtle's room. Had this diary been moved? But by whom? And where were the treasures that Constance mentioned? Surely they'd been found since then because all the family members were in the dollhouse. Or had they been replaced?

She decided to return one more time to examine the miniature people to see if there was a sign that they were newer than the rest of the dollhouse. *Twice in one day, I'm getting so clandestine.*

Elise tiptoed across the hall and snuck into Anna's room again. The bottom of the bookshelf beckoned with its unlocked secrets, making her mind spin. *One thing at a time here.* She walked to the window to push the curtains aside to allow in more light. Then, she turned toward the dollhouse, half in trepidation of discovering something else missing since her visit an hour earlier. *I don't think I can take any more.*

She carefully removed the little girl from the bed and looked her over. The doll's clothing had faded from years of little children's hands. Elise returned her and took out the father. His clothing was in a similar style and condition. There was nothing visible to prove that he wasn't the original doll either.

*So, they must have been found and returned, then.* Elise stepped back and studied the house as a whole. The top floor caught her attention. *That's right. The little room.* Standing on tiptoes, she studied the room in the back of the attic.

Just a plain little bed with the same dresser and an old fashioned wash basin that she remembered from the first time she'd seen it. But there was one new thing she hadn't remembered seeing before, a pair of slippers.

Nodding, Elise knew exactly who had slept there. Constance. She needed to get up there in that room. There had to be a clue of some sort where the diary had been kept.

But, it was going to be tricky without stairs. Charlotte had mentioned the entry way to the attic was in her room. Elise settled back to her feet and bit her thumbnail. *Do I dare? Just sneak in that room and check it out? What if I get caught?*

But wait. They were all preparing that big dinner tonight for Stephen's birthday. She wouldn't get caught.

Elise sidled out the door and down the hall to the stairwell where, after taking a big breath, she walked up the third-floor stairs acting like she belonged there. *Sure, I'm supposed to be here. What am I doing? Oh, just wanted to check out the laundry room with its dumbwaiter.* She smiled at how quickly she came up with a cover story. *Man, I need to add lying to my résumé.*

The bedrooms on the third floor were all marked with plain doors. She tried to orient herself by remembering where the laundry room was located. The first door opened to display a bed made up with a plain brown coverlet. Two pairs of men's shoes sat next to the wall. She hurriedly closed the door.

The next room had a feminine inhabitant but Elise quickly scanned the ceiling and didn't see a hatchway. She shut the door.

The third door opened to a bed covered with a calico quilt. Elise glanced at the ceiling and smiled at the sight of the rectangular opening. She glanced behind her to be sure no one was coming and entered the room.

Once inside, she studied the hatchway again, high above her head. Lovely. There was no way she could reach it, not even on her toes. She looked around the room for something to stand on and snagged the chair from the desk. After situating it underneath, she climbed up and looped her fingers under the handle and pulled. As it came down, cold air gushed from the open attic hole, making her shiver. She wished she'd thought to bring her cardigan but she wasn't going back for it now. Steeling herself with a couple deep breaths, she climbed up the ladder.

# Chapter 21

Elise climbed into the attic with her cell phone out as a flash light again. *Seriously, when I downloaded this flashlight app, I had no idea I'd be using it like this.* The beam bounced off of piles of clutter, that turned out to be chests and boxes, as her eyes adjusted to the darkness. Nothing weird so far. She climbed off the ladder and onto the floor.

The light from the phone danced off of the dark eyes of a toy doll, giving her a start. She flashed it around some more, catching a mannequin that stood next to a pile of boxes, a rocking horse with its tail half-eaten away, and several chairs in various stages of decay. The beam wasn't able to reach the other side of the attic, and she shivered at all of its hidden nooks. Charlotte's insistence of hearing something drag across the floor sent fear like fire through Elise's veins. She breathed in deeply. *Pull it together. Not a good time to think about that story.*

Pitch black couldn't even begin to describe how dark the attic was. The cell's light seemed to battle the darkness, making it feel as though the objects it landed on were jumping out at her. She swallowed several times to control her rising panic. *In and out. I can do this.*

There was no noise. In a way, the silence was worse, almost freakier to her ears than a noise. Every step she took seemed magnified. Even her tiptoes sounded like something horrific being dragged along the floor, and the echoes made her even jumpier.

According to the dollhouse, the little room was down to her left. Did her great, great grandma have to cross this dark expanse every night on her way to the room? The back of her neck tickled as though someone was watching her.

*You know what? I'm just going to fly through here. No big searches. Just thirty seconds tops.* With that goal, she scrambled to her left to search for a door.

Elise found it right away, as the beam glittered off the old door knob. The strangest feeling hit her when she grabbed the knob, almost as if she could see her great, great grandma grab it the same way.

*She slept here. Of course, she did this.* The door swung open before stopping half-way. The door's frame must have settled off center, causing the door to drag against the floor. She wiggled through and flashed the light around.

There was the bed. For some reason, a lump swelled in her throat thinking of young Constance sleeping up here all alone. There were the wash basin and the meager dresser.

Elise went to the dresser first and pulled on the drawer. It had swelled with moisture and wouldn't budge. The second one wiggled out a few inches before it jammed, too. The third was no better but was empty from what she could see.

She swept the light over by the bed. There it was. The brick wall behind the headboard. Getting down on her hands and knees, she looked under the bed, half expecting to see a pair of old slippers.

Mortar crumbled around the third brick from the bed post. Excitement buzzed through her, replacing any fear, as she wiggled under the bed. Carefully, she scraped at the edge of the brick until she had a grip and pulled it free. Nearly breathless with hope, she shone the light in the dark hole.

Empty.

*What in the? Who had been here?* She scooted out and sat there for moment. Someone had discovered this hiding place already, and it couldn't have been Anna since Constance hid it here the day the young teen had died.

Could it have been Myrtle?

Something clattered in the attic, making Elise's blood run cold. She froze and listened. *Dear God, help me! Did someone follow me up here? Do I turn off the light?* Her heart pounded in her chest. She tried to remember some of the self-defense moves from class. Slowly, she edged out of the door, listening.

There was no other sound. Light shown from the open hatchway like a portal to heaven. She raced for it, not caring any more if she made noise. All she wanted was to get down that ladder and out of the attic as fast as she could.

Charlotte's bed came into view below, and Elise almost cried in relief. Quickly, she slid down the ladder and into the maid's room. She wanted to kiss the ground. *How had Constance borne that every single night?* Without another moment wasted, she pushed the ladder up and shut the hatch door with a thump. She replaced the chair and quickly scanned the floor for any debris that might have fallen. Satisfied it was clear, she left the room. Her hands shook as she shut the door and hurried for the stairs.

Back in her bedroom, her thoughts raced around in no coherent pattern. She tried to sit but sprang up again, feeling jittery. *This is crazy. I've got to get out of here. Maybe go running.* She slipped on her hoodie and headed downstairs. No one saw her as she fled outdoors.

Jogging was just what she needed. By the time she made it to the end of the long driveway her adrenaline had been worked out and her thoughts started to make sense. But really, making sense was just another term for asking a string of questions. Because that was what was happening with each footfall. More and more questions.

But by the time she hit the end of the lane, the same person was becoming the focus of each question.

Stephen.

Why was Stephen back? Surely not for his birthday. He hadn't even planned to celebrate it with his mother.

Stephen ran her company with his sister.

Did Stephen discover the diary? He mentioned he'd heard the story of Anna many times. Had he decided to search out the room of the last nanny that had lived in the house?

Was his sister, Caroline, in on it too?

Elise frowned. Now each footfall was saying something different. Poor, poor Myrtle.

She jogged to the end of Old Parker's Road and turned down the main street. Shade from the large trees on the side of the road kept her cool, until she ran past the overgrown hedges where the sunlight hitting the pavement was brutal. She hardly noticed the heat with all the thoughts crammed in her head still needing to be recognized. So many questions. But, as many answers as Stephen's name filled, there was still a problem with him. He hadn't been in town when the gardener had been murdered.

Someone else must have done it. Someone close enough that they knew who Elise was. Knew when she was in or out of her room.

But whoever knew had never set off the trap she had on the doorknob of her room. Did they see the hair sitting there? Or did they come in at a different time.

*Like at night.* Electricity zipped up her spine at that thought. *No, there's no way. I lock the door at night.*

*Maybe they have a key.*

*No. I would hear them. I'm sure of it.*

The thought of Stephen's arrival date chafed at her. *Everything was clicking into place about him. That would have been perfect. But he came after I arrived.*

*Unless,* Elise's brain continue to argue with her, *he was already in town.* This was a possible explanation. After all, he had shown up earlier than Aunt Myrtle had expected.

*Maybe.*

Was there a way for her to find out when Stephen actually arrived? Would airports give out that kind of information? *I suppose I could check. Maybe I could text Brad and see if he has any ideas.* Her sneakers pounded the pavement and gave her the satisfaction that she was accomplishing something, even though she still was just as stuck as ever in the mystery. She hadn't jogged since she and Brad had run the half-marathon. *I've taken too long of a break. I love this. Why don't I keep up with it?* She jogged a mile further, enjoying the burn in her muscles as her thoughts turned toward the marathon. What an accomplishment that had been. From a couch potato to actually competing in a marathon. True, her time was nothing to brag about—she'd finished in the middle of the pack—but honestly, that beat her best expectation. Her only hope had been that she wouldn't trip and break a leg or something equally as embarrassing.

Brad had kept her company the entire time. He hadn't needed the same conditioning that she had needed. He stayed in shape for his job, and boy did it pay off the way he looked. She'd been so proud to have such a hot guy running next to *her*. *He chose me to run with.* She felt the same butterflies in her belly that she'd felt that day.

*Oh, Brad. It will be such a relief when you are finally home for good and we can figure out what's going on between us.* He really was an amazing guy, so patient and so funny. He actually listened to her when she talked like he wanted to hear what she had to say, so different from anything she'd ever experienced before. Her heart warmed at the thought of his sweet smile.

*I need to get my résumé going too. Aunt Myrtle's niece will be here soon, and this job really isn't working out for me anyway. It's making me appreciate and miss my home more than anything.* She turned around and jogged back to the lane. *There has to be something out there I qualify for. Maybe I should look into online classes and brush up on some office skills.*

Elise jogged past the forgotten homes and down Montgomery Manor's driveway. The huge maple trees loomed overhead. She glanced up at them and wondered at the stories they would share if they were able to speak. The things they must have seen. Little Myrtle on her bike. Mr. Montgomery coming home with his coins. Maybe even Anna's boyfriend?

Elise jogged past the garage and then past her little Pinto that looked so out of place in this environment. Even though the floral landscaping was overgrown, it was still impressive, and her yellow rusty car parked right in the middle was an embarrassment. She was surprised that Aunt Myrtle hadn't asked her to move it behind the garage. Her steps slowed as her breath came out in huffs. *What's that on my hood?* She walked over to examine it, trying to catch her breath.

Her first thoughts was that it was something dark but a bit sparkly. Suddenly, she recognized what it was and her heart leaped to her throat.

The replica doll of her was stabbed with a knife into the hood of her car.

She glanced around the front yard. There was no one to be seen. Scanning the ground, she looked for footsteps. *Don't be silly. The ground is dry, and it would nearly be impossible to leave anything.* There did seem to be some grass bent down near her car, maybe by the person who had stood there and jammed the knife.

She studied the knife sticking out of the doll's chest and shivered. *The force it must have taken to go through the doll and into the metal.* Unconsciously, she rubbed her own breast bone as she studied the knife. It looked like the same one they'd used with the turkey at lunch today. Deep in thought, her tongue darted across her bottom lip. Did it look like it had been twisted to the left? Nodding, she sprung into action, opening the car door and yanking open the glove box for a napkin. Using the napkin, she carefully pried the knife free, wincing at the noise it made as she worked it back and forth. When it was finally free in her hand, she locked both it and the doll in her trunk. She slammed the lid shut and stared at the house.

Now, she knew who had killed the gardener.

# Chapter 22

Elise reached into her pocket to call the police. Crap! In her jitteriness earlier, she'd left without her phone. She didn't want to run all the way back upstairs. Instead, she needed to check out her theory before someone came along and destroyed the evidence. Even though it was only three-thirty, it was already getting dark. Elise hurried around the side of the house and came out into the back yard. She skirted the outside of the maze hedge and headed for the woods behind the property.

The same woods that lay between Uncle Shorty's estate and Montgomery Manor.

Her hope that there might be a clear cut path quickly withered at the sight of the underbrush and fallen leaves. Still, there were only a few acres between the two properties. She was confident that she'd find what she was looking for.

Boulders covered in moss lay all around her. *Where did they come from? Was this an old river bed?* She skirted an old stump—four feet tall by nearly as wide, but obviously crumbled with age—and wondered if the Manor's kids had come out here to play. Perhaps played king of the hill on this very spot?

The trees around her thinned, revealing a bank running along the opposite side. She looked up at a tree, one of the largest around and covered in hanging moss. Near the top, it had split into three thick boughs like ogre fingers. *This has to be it.*

She spun backward and searched for the cave in the embankment. *Yes! There it is.* One of the tree's boughs butted up nearly against it. The tree must have grown quite a bit because there was no need for a rope bridge now.

*It still doesn't change the fact that the branch is thirty feet off the ground.*

*Or that someone died falling from there.*

*Am I going to do it?* She shook out her hands and started to jump up and down to warm up her arms and legs.

*Yep. I guess I'm crazy like that.*

She took a running leap and caught hold of the lowest branch. Her feet pedaled, like she was on a bicycle, until she scrambled up. She pulled closer to the trunk, a trunk so wide she couldn't dream of reaching around it even if Lavina had been on the other side reaching back towards her. The tree was a behemoth, and its bark was riddled with woodpecker holes, various insects, and an ant trail marching around the jags in its surface. She looked up and swallowed. *Get moving, missy. That branch just isn't going to reach down and pluck you up.*

Clinging to the trunk, Elise got to her feet. She reached for the next branch, this one closer and just a step away. She grabbed hold of it and grimaced at the wad of sap she'd somehow found. With a lot of grunting and groaning, she pulled herself up.

The next branch was easier, but as Elise stood on it she heard a crack. The limb trembled, and Elise along with it. Looking up, she quickly lunged for the next.

Slowly, she made her way up the side of the tree. Her breathing sounded like a locomotive and her arms ached. *How much farther?* She balanced against the trunk and brushed the hair from her sweaty face, her nose wrinkling as the hair stuck to the sap. She glanced up, squinting as tiny things fell from above. *Just a little bit more. I'm almost there.*

Finally, she was at the ogre fingers, two pointing to the sky and one pointing at the cave. She'd have to crawl along this one like a snake. She closed her eyes and prayed it would hold her weight and gradually crept out.

The tip of the branch bobbled with a swish of leaves as she crawled. Her stomach was tight with knots. She slipped and grabbed the limb just as tightly. Her own adrenaline was making her shake so much it was hard to keep balance. *Don't look down. Whatever you do. Just look straight ahead. Almost there.*

Inch by inch, she crept along the branch. After what felt like an eternity, she was at the cave's lip. Holding her breath, she slid her foot down onto it and climbed off as if she were dismounting a horse.

This was it. This was what she'd been searching for the entire time.

Anna's lair.

Elise reached for her cell phone from her back pocket, groaning slightly when she realized she'd left it behind. *It is what it is.* Fortunately, light from the afternoon sun splashed against the rock's surface at the entrance and brightened the whole cave. The walls were covered in paintings of flowers. Little blobs of peeling yellow for dandelions. Red for roses. A rotting blanket lay folded on the floor, and next to that, a miniature table with a darkly smudged plate that must have held pretend food at one time.

Elise felt a lump rise in her throat. It was a young girl's fort. Anna was only fifteen when she died, caught between the whimsy of childhood and the threshold of adulthood.

She picked away across the cave's floor to the back, her eyes narrowing. One thing was missing. Where was the hiding place for the stuff that Anna liked to steal?

Brushing the hair back from her face, she crouched and examined the back. As far as she could tell, it was a solid rock surface.

Elise took a step back, and her eyebrows knotted together. The floor felt funny. She bounced up and down before kneeling to sweep at the dirt. After a few minutes, she'd uncovered a wooden board. Excitement danced in her heart as she pried it up.

Underneath was a hollow filled with cigar boxes. Rows and rows of them. She reached in and pulled out the first box. As she opened it, sadness filled her when the lid tore away at its paper hinges. Inside was a paint set. The bristles had long ago disappeared off the wooden paint brushes. She set the box to one side and opened the next.

A gasp ripped from her throat. It was filled to the brim with silver coins. She opened the next and the next, twelve boxes in all, and they were all the same.

Her brain couldn't do the math quickly enough. But, at ten thousand dollars a coin, she was looking at over several million dollars, she was sure. The shock of it hit her like a punch and she staggered back a few steps. All this time…just sitting here.

Reaching into her pocket, she pulled out the coin she found earlier and flipped it into the pile. It tinked before sliding to a stop. *I've got to tell somebody, like right now.* Her face flushed with excitement, she turned back to the entrance.

*Okay hurry, but don't hurry. I don't want to die out here.*

A rope fell from up high and pooled on the cave floor. She looked up, stunned. Dirt sifted down along with a few rocks.

With a thump, a man in a black mask slid down and landed in front of her.

# Chapter 23

"Well, now. If it isn't little Miss Snoopy. Put your hands up."

The voice was oddly familiar. The voice from the phone. And the same voice she knew somewhere else.

Elise looked at him with her hands in the air. "Hello, Dave," she said.

She'd faced him before, but that was different. That was with the whole class chanting encouragement on her behalf, and Dave looking slightly bemused.

He pulled off the mask, no longer looking bemused. In fact, deadly would be a better term, with the hard lines creasing around his mouth. She clenched her fists and brought them to her side, trying to remember what, oddly enough, he had taught her. *Aim for the nose, the throat, the eyes, the groin. Scrape down the shin.*

His lip twisted into a wry grin and his fingers flicked at her, beckoning her to move closer. "Sure, come on at me. You forget that I'm the one who showed you all those moves. I know how to defend against them, too."

She kept her arms loose and relaxed. "Does your grandfather know who you really are?"

"Oh, you've come late to the party. You think it's just me? We're all working together over there." Horror filled her at his words. "There's no one who's coming to your aid, Missy. Not a single soul."

"Wha—What do you mean?"

He pulled a pair of gloves from his pocket and casually put them on. "Who do you think told me to follow you today? A little bird?" He smirked. "A bird sure did. My girlfriend, Charlotte."

A whimper escaped Elise.

"And, who do you think let me in on this little treasure hunt to begin with?"

"Her son?" The words fell out numbly out of her mouth.

"Stephen? No, he's being fleeced the same as the old lady. It was dear old Mr. Hamilton. He hired me to intimidate the gardener, and in return, he was going to let me in on some of the silver booty." Dave arched an eyebrow at the cigar boxes behind her. "Of course, we had no idea where it was, so thank you for finding it for us."

Elise took a small step to the left. His words were like punches, each one knocking her off guard. "What do you mean, intimidate? Seems like he's dead."

Dave laughed and glanced to the left. *Just one big push and I could.... Oh my gosh, could I kill him? Could I do it?* He clenched his hands and the rubber gloves squeaked. *I have to, or he'll kill me first.*

"I may have gone a tad too far in my intimidation. But Hamilton already owed me money at that point. And I wanted to make sure I got paid."

"Why would Hamilton do that?" She took another small step to the left, trying to look like she was just shifting in place.

"You don't know? You, the greatest snoop of all couldn't figure it out?" He pulled on the tips of his glove and then intersected his fingers to tighten them. "Why, he's Anna's old beau, the most revengeful man I know. He's just been biding his time, using his job to torture poor Myrtle into thinking her sister's been haunting her all these years. I think it was almost a side note for him to search for the silver."

"What did the gardener have to do with it?"

"Wow, you find the money and don't know a thing about anything else. And here, we know everything and we've just been spinning our tires in search for the coins all these years." He shook his head. "The gardener was Hamilton's cousin. They've been in on it all these years, ever since they saw Mr. Montgomery bring home the coins. He'd given the two of them one as a celebration for the war's end. Recently, Hamilton got bitten by the dragon spell and was convinced his cousin had already found the coins and was holding out on him. Hamilton wanted me to shake him up a bit." Dave raised his eyebrows. "I guess I sure did."

With no warning, Dave rushed at her and grabbed her around her neck. She turned her chin towards his elbow to keep him from crushing her throat. She jerked her arm down and he blocked it, expecting a groin punch.

He wasn't paying attention to her other hand. She reached back with her fingers stiff and straight and jabbed him as hard as she could in his eye. Immediately, he released her with a scream. He clawed at his face, for a moment, as blood poured from his eye socket.

Without looking to see what he would do next, she darted past him and dove for the branch.

It bounced under her weight. Quickly, she wiggled across. Her horror doubled as the branch shuddered mightily again. He had jumped too and was crawling after her. She crept as fast as she could, the forest floor spinning dizzily under her. A hand grabbed her foot but she was able to kick free. Once at the trunk, she stood, and jumped down to the next branch, nearly missing it. She caught it across her stomach and the bark scraped against her bare skin from where her shirt ripped up.

Cracking overhead told her he wasn't far behind. She swung her feet and made it to the next branch, and before she was completely balanced, she dropped to the next.

The last branch was six feet off the ground. Steeling herself for the impact, she dropped to the dirt.

Elise stumbled forward a few steps before getting her footing. She raced ahead as sounds of him landing came right behind her. Her heart was in her throat, she couldn't breathe, her legs felt like rubber but she didn't care. *Run! Run! Run!*

It didn't take her long before she could hear he was gaining on her. She started to search for a weapon even as her feet flew across the ground. She dodged the boulders. *I'm almost there! Almost out!*

Almost? There was no one safe to help her at the house. No one.

She was going to have to face this alone.

He was getting closer. She could hear his feet scraping against the leaves and cracking the branches. But she could hear him panting, too. He was getting gassed out.

*I can do this. I can get away.*

Her foot rolled across a rock and she nearly fell, but caught herself against a tree. He was right behind her. She felt the sweep of his fingertips on her arm as he lunged for her.

Then, she saw it in front of her. A perfectly shaped branch, maybe an old walking stick, that looked like it had been placed right there just for her. Without missing a beat, she picked it up and swung it around like a bat.

CRACK! It connected with his jaw. His eyes rolled back into his head and he fell bonelessly to the ground. Shaking, she walked over to him, ready to hit him again. When she was sure he was unconscious, she reached for her phone to dial 911.

A weight like a thousand bricks hit her as she realized she'd left it behind. *There's nothing for it. I'll have to go back. Let's just take care of this.* She ripped the laces out of her shoe and, grunting, rolled him onto his face. With her muscles on fire from the effort, she pulled his heavy arms behind his back and tied them. She started to unlace her other shoe but, suddenly, she felt so tired. Completely drained. She just wanted to sit and to not move again for a year. *Oh, man. If my bed was here I'd crawl in right now and not give a crap about any ghosts ever again.*

Finally, she unlaced it and tied his feet together.

Stumbling, she made for the Manor. Her body felt like it had been beaten by 2x4's. She slipped through the French doors of the living room and headed for the kitchen. Cookie looked at her questionably as she entered, but Elise didn't offer an explanation. Instead, she grabbed the ancient phone off the receiver and dialed 911.

After the call, Elise gave a threatening glare to Cookie. "Sit," she told the cook, stabbing her finger towards the chair.

Cookie waddled over, brushing down her apron nervously. Elise collapsed in the chair across from her, wanting to rest her head on the table. She didn't dare, not without knowing who was friend or foe in the house.

It wasn't long before Elise heard the sirens. Another few minutes and five or six of them filed in through the kitchen, all of them with their guns drawn. Hamilton trailed behind them, calling out impotently, "Hey now. What's this about?"

"You guys are a sight for sore eyes," Elise said weakly, having made her way to the front door. She led them out the French doors and pointed to where Dave still lay unconscious. Cautiously, they made their way over to him, only holstering their guns when they saw he wasn't going anywhere.

"Anyone else around that you know of?" One officer asked Elise, who'd followed them up the hill. He pulled out his handcuffs and secured Dave.

"He mentioned there were others at the house that were working with him. Hamilton, the butler, Charlotte, the house keeper. I'm not sure if there are more."

The officers had her stay outside while they returned to the house to take those two into custody. Seeing Elise shivering, one officer brought her a blanket.

Lavina arrived as the excitement wound down, stalking across the lawn in a panic in high heeled shoes.

"Elise!" she yelled. "Elise, are you okay?"

Elise smiled at her as Lavina approached. "Never better."

"Oh, my heavens! You're bleeding!" Her best friend grabbed her in a hug, and they both collapsed. And Elise couldn't lie, she kind of collapsed emotionally too.

# Chapter 24

That night, Elise and Lavina crammed into the window seat of the library. Elise was still chilled to the bones and huddled under a quilt trying to get warm. Her face felt quilt-like too, with its crosshatch of band-aids from her trip down the tree. Aunt Myrtle sat across from them and quietly rocked in her chair.

The fire crackled in the fireplace and made dancing shadows around the room.

Elise sighed, as the heat finally started to soak in.

"You okay, darlin'?" Lavina asked.

"I'm fine. Tired."

"Well, you should be. You shook everything up around here," declared Aunt Myrtle. She scowled at the flames. "And made me worried about you, too."

Elise knew what she meant. That was a fond compliment coming from Aunt Myrtle.

"How is Stephen? Upset about his birthday dinner being ruined?"

Aunt Myrtle took a sip of her tea and ignored her by saying, "Lavina Sue, I do declare tonight calls for a bit of brandy. Now, just hop up and get me a splash, will you?"

Lavina laughed under her breath as she stood from the seat to do Aunt Myrtle's bidding. She tipped some into Aunt Myrtle's teacup, then poured two more swishes in a couple of glasses and carried them back to the window seat. "I should have thought of this earlier," Lavina said, handing Elise her glass. "Sip it. You'll be warm in no time."

Elise took a sip and coughed. She covered her mouth and looked up at her friend who was laughing at her. "Shut up."

"Watch your tongue!" Aunt Myrtle barked. "And, about Stephen, well he couldn't have cared two hoots about dinner. That young man had a meeting with another bank. Apparently, the Manor hasn't been doing as well as I thought, and he's been worried these last few years, trying to think of how to make enough money to save the house." Aunt Myrtle snorted. "He should have just come to me and not treated me as though I have duck fluff for brains."

Elise took another sip, this one going down easier. "How did you know where the Freedom dollars were, Aunt Myrtle?"

"Oh, child, I knew where those coins were all these years. Papa used to hide them himself in fake books, in the bookshelf, in his room. Heck, I watched Anna pilfer half of those coins up there. She never knew I followed her. That Anna always had trouble with taking things that didn't belong to her. It was like an addiction. She couldn't resist a shiny object. She took everything; silverware, Mother's perfume, Papa's coins. Over time, I just got used to sneaking up there to the cave and hauling things back so no one would notice they were missing."

Aunt Myrtle sighed. "And I never got caught by her. Until the last time when I popped out. I thought we could share the secret. I never realized how much it made her ashamed. I think it shamed her when she saw me there." Aunt Myrtle twisted her fingers together, making Elise wince at the harsh treatment of the woman's knobby knuckles. "After she fell," Aunt Myrtle's voice dropped. "And I knew she was gone, I searched her pockets and took back the miniature lamp and vase that she'd swiped. I didn't want anyone to know."

Lavina stared at the floor, while Elise studied the liquid in her cup, both listening. "We love you, Aunt Myrtle," Lavina whispered.

The old woman glanced up at them, and a small smile fluttered over her mouth. "And I love you, too. But don't tell anyone I said that. I'll never admit to such hogwash sappiness."

The two young women laughed.

"So," Aunt Myrtle took another sip. "That Hamilton was Anna's beau, huh? Worked for me all those years and never let on how angry he was at me."

Elise nodded. "Anna is at peace. It was never her stealing things from you or from the dollhouse."

"Well, I don't know about that. Hard to teach an old dog new tricks. There's a piece of me that kind of wishes it was, and maybe I'll just decide to believe it was so."

The quiet descended over the room again as Anna played on their thoughts. Finally, Aunt Myrtle sighed and struggled for her cane. "Well, I'm going to bed," she said and stood up unsteadily. She straightened her cardigan draped over her shoulders and slowly thumped out of the room.

"That is the first time Aunt Myrtle offered me a drink," Lavina murmured.

"I'm not sure she really did. I think you just took it." Elise hiccuped.

Lavina turned to look at her with concerned eyes. "My good gracious, are you buzzed?"

Elise laughed. "Maybe a tiny bit."

Lavina rolled her eyes. "You're going to be useless to answer my questions."

"Nonsense," Elise argued. "Ask away."

"So, why were the things from the dollhouse taken?"

"Hamilton was trying to haunt Aunt Myrtle. He'd been doing it for years. Back when he first got a position here, he started stealing baby clothes. Anything he could do to ruin her happiness and never let her have a moment of peace."

"What a dirt bag."

"Yeah, he was. I think the last real advocate Aunt Myrtle had was Constance. My great, great grandma adored her." Elise bit her lip in deep thought. "But I'm pretty sure Aunt Myrtle was the one who found Constance's diary. Hopefully, it comforted her to know how much Constance cared."

"It's just so bizarre how your relative took care of her when she was young, and here you are now taking care of her." Elise nodded as Lavina continued, "You said when you got back to the Manor you knew who had murdered the gardener. How did you know it was Dave?"

Elise shook her head. "It was the weirdest hunch. When I saw the knife stabbed into the hood at that angle it reminded me of how he'd done a knife demonstration at class. And then it clicked where I'd seen him before. It was the day I was exploring the maze. He was in there too, checking out the hole the gardener had dug. Both Hamilton and Dave had been suspicious that the gardener had found the silver already."

"Hamilton was in on it with the gardener too?"

"Yeah, they were actually cousins. In fact, Dave alluded to it when we were at class, probably thumbing his nose at the both of us. Remember when he said practically everyone was related up there?"

"That jackknob. Who else is related?"

"I think that's all. I know Charlotte was his girlfriend. At least, he told her that, probably using her to gain information about the house. I don't foresee that he would have stayed with her, once the money had been found. Dave was desperate for money to support his exercise studio. He was having a hard time keeping it afloat."

"What about the shoes? I remember you telling me about shoes that were missing."

"Not missing, mismatched. Either Hamilton or Charlotte tried to scare Aunt Myrtle with the shoe prints through her room. Apparently the paint, or whatever it was didn't come off, and it was just carelessness that they replaced them with a different size."

Elise got quiet for a moment before blurting out, "And that's another thing, Aunt Myrtle's room has French doors. People most likely have been coming in and out of the house unseen for years through her room and the connecting hidden passageway."

"Hidden...?" Lavina looked at her with one perfectly plucked eyebrow raised.

Elise sighed. "Honestly, I'm exhausted now. I'll tell you more about it later."

Matilda tapped on the library door before poking her head in. "I'm sorry to disturb you ladies, but someone is here to see you, Ms. Pepper."

Directly behind the housekeeper was the best thing Elise had ever seen. Brad.

Lavina took a quick glance at him before standing up and placing her cup on the table. "Well, on that note, I'll say goodbye." She gave her friend a hug before sidling passed Brad with a nod of her red head.

Brad hurried over to Elise and grabbed her in his arms. "Woman, you're going to be the death of me."

She snuggled in, breathing in his spicy cologne. "Brad! What are you doing here? What about your training?"

"Tomorrow is just paperwork, which I've already finished. I'll have to go back for one more weekend, but it was worth getting out to see you." He groaned and buried his face in her shoulder. "I just can't believe I talked you into taking a safety course with that creep."

"You couldn't have known. And trust me, it helped. Thank you." She tickled his chin until he looked up.

Brad reached over and tucked a stray hair behind her ear. "Well, I'm super proud of you. My little kung-fu hero."

Elise smiled, feeling all warm inside. "Me too, actually. I really overcame something during that class. Something I never thought I would."

"Just don't be thinking you can go around kicking bad guys to the ground any time you want." He lowered his eyebrows and gave her a pretend scowl.

She laughed. "You got it."

"Which reminds me, what are you thinking about the future?"

"The future?" Her cheeks started hurting from the big grin she was trying to hold in.

"Yeah." His hand slipped down her arm until he held hers. He gave it a gentle squeeze. "With me."

the end

Thank you for reading The Sour Taste of Suspicion. Please check out the rest of the Angel Lake series; The Sweet Taste of Murder and The Bitter Taste of Betrayal.

Follow me at CeeCee James, author, on Facebook for new books and free give-aways!

Made in the USA
San Bernardino,
CA

58801256R00134